"You're in real danger."

Daniel speared her with a glance as he continued, "This sounds like a bad movie, but I assure you, those men weren't actors."

"You mean my...father is a killer?"

"Killing is merciful compared to what his men do."

Katie shook her head, wrapping her arms tightly around her torso. *I can't deal with this.*

Daniel reached for her, compassion in his eyes. "The truth–"

"Truth?" Katie snorted, anger rising above her reasoning. "Tell me, Daniel, was the loss of my mother not enough? Why would you think I could handle news like this right now?" She slammed the dashboard with her fist. "I want off this insanity ride. Take me home now."

"I'm sorry. I can't do that."

The endless sight line of fields, cows and highway blurred behind Katie's frustrated tears, but she refused to allow them to fall. "Then what happens now?"

"We get to the ranch. Then in the morning, we fly out."

"Do I get an opinion?"

"Not if you want to live."

Sharee Stover is a Colorado native transplanted to Nebraska, where she lives with her husband, three children and two dogs. Her mother instilled in her the love of books before Sharee could read, along with the promise "If you can read, you can do anything." When she's not writing, she enjoys time with her family, long walks with her obnoxiously lovable German shepherd and crocheting. Find her at shareestover.com or on Twitter, @shareestover.

Books by Sharee Stover

Love Inspired Suspense

Secret Past

Secret Past

Sharee Stover

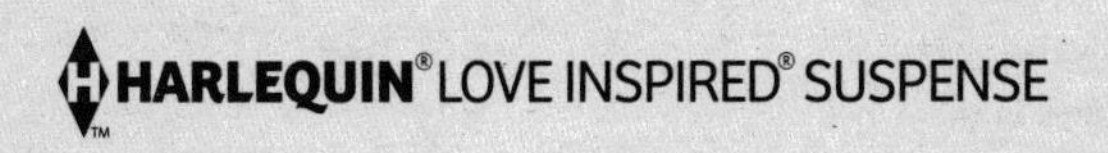

Recycling programs for this product may not exist in your area.

LOVE INSPIRED BOOKS

ISBN-13: 978-1-335-54372-1

Secret Past

This edition published by arrangement with Love Inspired Books.

www.Harlequin.com

Printed in U.S.A.

For nothing is secret, that shall not be made manifest;
neither any thing hid, that shall not be known
and come abroad.

—*Luke* 8:17

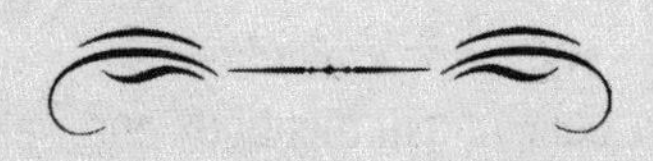

For Jim, my real-life hero, and my children,
Tawny, Cody and Andi. My cup runneth over
every single day because of you. Thank you for giving
me the courage and support to pursue my dreams.

Also, many thanks to:

My editor, Emily Rodmell.
Thank you for believing in this book and welcoming me
into the Love Inspired Suspense family.
It's a dream come true.

My mentors, Tina Radcliffe, Mary Connealy,
Rachel Dylan and Joy Avery Melville. Thank you
for always keeping it real, surrounding me
with your prayers and encouragement,
and for imparting your words of wisdom.

My writing sisters and critique partners, Connie Queen,
Jackie Layton and Rhonda Starnes. Thank you
for those endless hours of reading and critiquing.

Most important, thank You, Jesus, for making me Yours.
All glory and honor belong to You.

ONE

Uncle Nick is going to kill me.

Katie traced her mother's picture in Starling, Nebraska's Thursday morning edition of the *Stars Gazette*. Her heart squeezed at the sight of Mama's healthy precancer smile and the newspaper's eloquently compiled full-page obituary tribute.

Outside, car doors slammed. *He's here.*

She should feel guilty for disobeying her uncle's instructions but how could she? The editor had done a stellar job of emphasizing the town's appreciation and love for Mama. The photo was a normal part of the memorial.

The front door burst open, and Uncle Nick stormed in shaking a fisted newspaper. "Katherine Tribani, how dare you defy me this way!"

And the battle continues. She pushed herself to a sitting position on the couch. Piles of used tissues fluttered to the floor, and she leaned over to pick them up. "I tried to cancel…"

Her gaze landed on the stranger who trailed her enraged uncle. The tall, muscular man dressed in all black gave a terse nod before closing the door, sending a wave of crisp autumn air to her.

The early morning sunlight beamed through the picture window, bouncing off her uncle's bald head. "I told you not to give the *Gazette* any pictures of your mother." Nick rushed to the curtains, pulling them closed.

"I'm sorry." *Not really.* "They'd already printed it by the time I got a hold of anyone." Katie spoke in the calmest voice she could muster, though her ears burned hot with embarrassment at his berating.

Aware of her disheveled appearance, she stood and combed her fingers through the tangles in her long hair. Grabbing another tissue, she wiped her cheeks. There was nothing she could do about the puffiness of her eyes. Three days of crying had taken their toll.

"Why couldn't you obey me, just this once?" Nick's cowboy boots clomped in rhythm to his ranting, muffled briefly as he circled between the hardwood floors and red throw rug. "—no idea what you've done..."

Her gaze shifted between the stranger and Nick, who still clutched and shook the newspaper in time with his words. He tossed the periodical at her feet.

Katie studied the visitor who appeared to survey the room from his position against the door. He wore a black dri-fit shirt, cargo pants and military boots accessorized by a gun holstered on his hip. Nick carried, so it wasn't like she hadn't seen guns. Most just weren't as publicly displayed. Quiet and controlled, the man's demeanor said he was in the armed forces or law enforcement. No visible badge. Why would her uncle bring a cop here? His presence was intimidating, intriguing and vaguely familiar. Had he been at the funeral?

"Did you even read the tribute?" Katie squatted, smoothing the crumpled newspaper on the glass coffee table. She bit back her smart retort, *I'm twenty-five years old and don't need your permission.* Nick's temper wasn't something to counter.

"Of course I read the story and saw the picture. You have no idea what kind of danger you've put yourself in." Nick stomped down the hallway.

Katie started after him. "Danger? Don't be silly." Her uncle's paranoia wasn't new, but his frenzy was unnerving.

The stranger took two long strides, halting her with a touch to the shoulder. He gave a slight shake of his head. "Grab anything you can't live without." As if that explained everything.

She met his gaze. "Who are you?"

"He's your new handler. US Marshal Daniel Knight," Nick interrupted, returning to the living room. "He'll take you to the safe house."

"Marshal? Uncle Nick. Stop." Katie shook her head, questions tumbling out of her mouth faster than either man could respond. "New? When did I have an old one? What's a handler? Why do I need a safe house?"

A look passed between the men.

"Uncle Nick, I can't deal with your craziness today. Take your friend and let me grieve the loss of my mother." Katie snatched the scattered tissues from the floor and stormed to the kitchen, shoving them into the trash can. Straightening her hoodie over her favorite jeans, she returned to the living room.

"Katherine, we're running out of time." Nick rubbed his forehead. A classic sign of his frustration.

Katie clamped her mouth shut and folded her arms across her chest, staring at Nick.

"For the past twenty years, you and your mother have been under witness protection. Your mother's real name is Evangelina Marino. The wife of Anthony Marino. A convicted crime lord," Daniel explained.

Her gaze flitted to the handsome guest. "Stop there. My mother's name was Maggie. She would never marry someone like that."

"Katherine." Nick's warning hung in her name.

Katie blew out a breath. "Fine, I'm listening." Her uncle was out of his paranoid mind if he thought she was buying this story.

Nick continued. "Evangelina went into WITSEC after testifying against Marino. He should've served a life sentence, but his sleazy attorney is skilled at red tape and games. Marino was recently released. We'd been able to stay under the radar until—" He gestured toward the newspaper.

Tires squealed outside.

Daniel rushed to the window, peeking through a corner of the curtains. “They’re here.”

He kept watch on the mysterious visitors as Nick jumped up, drew Katie into a hug and pulled her toward the kitchen. He pressed something into her hand and whispered against her ear, “Take this. Hide it. No matter what happens, don’t let anyone know you have it.”

“Uncle Nick. I—”

He gave a slight nod, and she slipped the item into her jeans pocket.

“Daniel will explain the rest.” Nick pulled the Glock he always carried from inside his jacket. “Katherine, go with Daniel. Do whatever he says. No arguments.”

Katie gasped. “But…”

Nick’s look silenced her. He turned to Daniel. “Go out the kitchen door. Get your vehicle from my house and take her to the ranch. I’ll hold them off and meet you there.”

Car doors slammed followed by men’s voices.

“Who’s—” In one swift motion, Daniel threw Katie over his shoulder, blood rushing to her head. Her stomach pressed against his shoulder, whooshing the breath from her chest.

Daniel took two strides through the kitchen and out of the house. The metal blinds over the windowed door smacked behind them.

Katie’s inverted position gave her a too-close

view of the ground as he carried her out the door and through the pristine backyard.

Mama's bright orange-and-yellow chrysanthemums, planted at the edge of the unfenced yard, grazed her outstretched hand.

A series of pops like muffled fireworks emitted from inside. The little brick house faded from sight.

She craned her neck. Daniel bolted down the alley, behind Mrs. Pauley's home, eliminating her view.

"Put. Me. Down," Katie huffed.

Daniel's rhythmic breathing matched his gait.

The quiet neighborhood was oblivious to her early-morning madness. Where was nosy Mrs. Pauley when you needed her? Probably not even awake yet.

She bounced against Daniel's back with each step until nausea threatened. He whipped around the block, sliding Katie off his shoulder. She held her stomach. They stood at the corner of Wicker and Acacia. Nick's street.

Katie swayed in place. Her gaze focused past Daniel's massive frame. She could run. Mr. Yonker was always home. He'd hear her scream.

"Don't even think about it." Daniel tugged her toward Nick's house. "Keep up."

She wouldn't defy Nick…again. *Please, God, don't let Daniel be a psychopath.*

The red-brick bungalow was a cookie-cutter

replica of her mother's home. Typical of Starling's simple architecture.

An unfamiliar black Suburban with dark-tinted windows was parked in Nick's driveway. Definitely out of place.

Daniel aimed a key fob at the vehicle and released his hold on her. "Get in."

The engine roared to life as she ran to the passenger side and jumped in. Daniel sped in Reverse out of the driveway and onto the street before Katie could get her seat belt latched.

"You're going back for Uncle Nick, right?" She leaned forward, bracing herself against the dashboard.

Rays of sunshine pierced through the windshield as Daniel turned east onto the county road. He slipped on a pair of slim, high-wrap sunglasses.

She smacked the dashboard. "Hello, you're going the wrong way."

Daniel didn't respond.

"Did you hear me? We have to go back."

The engine revved.

A pinging sounded behind them.

Katie twisted around. "What was that?"

"Hang on." Daniel jerked the wheel.

Katie slid toward the door. She gripped the seat, righting herself, and caught a glimpse in her side mirror.

A black sedan pursued. A man leaned out of the passenger side, aiming a gun at them.

"There's a man with a gun." She faced Daniel.

Her mind raced. Guns were familiar; being shot at was not.

Daniel checked the rearview and side mirrors, swerving as a barrage of bullets showered the vehicle. A moving target was harder to hit. Great in theory, except Nebraska's topography wasn't known for its many curves and turns as confirmed by the long stretch of straight road looming ahead.

"Who's shooting at us?"

"Put your foot on the accelerator and steer." He opened his window, inviting a blast of cool air.

Katie gripped his arm. "What're you doing?"

No time for details. "I need to return fire. Take the wheel and keep us on the road."

She released her hold and Daniel prepared for an argument. Instead, Katie inched across the front seat, placing her foot against the accelerator. The vehicle lurched forward.

"Sorry."

"Got it?" Daniel moved his hands from the wheel, giving her reign. He withdrew his Glock from the holster and leaned out the window, firing several rounds at the sedan.

Two bullets pierced the driver's side windshield. The vehicle veered to the shoulder then back to the lane, recovering pursuit.

Daniel ducked as the shooter responded with

a staccato procession of gunshots, shattering the Suburban's back window.

"Hang on!" Katie warned.

He twisted around. A massive green tractor with spray booms stretched across the two-lane highway. The monstrosity moved at a sloth's pace in front of them while a semi sped closer in the oncoming lane.

Katie swerved to the left, into the oncoming lane around the machinery. She overcalculated and lost traction as they fishtailed on the loose gravel of the shoulder.

Daniel clung to the doorframe. "Are you crazy? You're going to kill me before they do." He flattened his body against the cab as Katie whipped back into her lane, narrowly missing the semi.

"Then let me shoot and you drive," she snapped.

A grin tugged at his lips at the feisty retort, and he shifted to deal with their pursuers.

"I can't outrun them."

"Just keep it steady."

The sedan attempted to mimic Katie's tractor-passing maneuver, but the driver underestimated the closing speed of the oncoming semi. Just before impact, the driver jerked the car to the left. Daniel anticipated the result, watching with satisfaction as the car dipped into the ditch then went airborne, rolling several times before coming to rest on its top.

He slapped the door. "Let me back in."

Katie slowed the vehicle, and they made the exchange.

"Good job," he commended, accelerating.

"Who was that? Why are they trying to kill us?"

Great, here come the questions. "Anthony Marino's men."

"Daniel, I realize you're in a bad position, but I need more information." Katie leaned forward.

He grimaced.

Her emerald eyes bored through him. "You said Mama and I have been in witness protection for twenty years?"

"More than twenty," Daniel inserted.

"Okay. Starling's got a population of fewer than two thousand people. It's not even on most maps."

Daniel checked the rearview mirror, stalling. "The internet's an intrusive thing."

Katie covered her mouth with her hand. "*That's* why Uncle Nick demanded Mama's picture be left out of the *Gazette*'s tribute. They published the story in print and on their website."

He nodded, grateful she'd pieced it together.

Katie's shoulders slumped. "I thought he was being eccentric. He hated social media, really anything that involved the internet."

"He knew if the picture ever got out on the World Wide Web, Marino would find a way to locate you all. With technology like facial recognition software, it was only a matter of time."

"Why didn't Nick or Mama tell me the truth? I wouldn't have given the newspaper Mama's picture if I'd known all of this."

Daniel worked his jaw. Funny, isn't that what he'd told Garrett too? "We argued about that more than once." He avoided Katie's penetrating gaze, focusing on the road.

"I still don't understand how this has anything to do with me. If Mr. Marino was angry at Mama, he's too late to do anything about it. She's already..." Katie's voice hitched, and she turned, facing the passenger window.

"We believe Marino's intention is to kidnap you."

"But I don't know anything. None of this makes sense. Why on earth would the man want me?"

Might as well give her the full reveal. "Your mother committed the ultimate sin in Marino's world. Not only did she betray him with her testimony, she took away his most precious possession. He's vowed to pursue everything he lost."

Katie shifted. "Whatever this precious item is, if it means enough for him to kill, he can have the stupid thing. Then this nightmare will be over."

If only it were that easy. "Marino doesn't want a thing. He wants a person."

"That's dumb. He can't have a person."

"People are possessions to Marino. Things he can own and treat however he chooses. He's a narcissist."

"No wonder Mama wanted to get away from him," Katie mumbled. "Who's this person he wants to own?"

Daniel swallowed, staring out of the windshield. "You."

"Why me?" Her green eyes widened.

Spit it out, Knight. "Because you're Anthony Marino's daughter."

TWO

Daniel's words hung between them, a cloud of fog and distance. Katie couldn't tear her gaze away. He had to be joking. A cruel and stupid joke, but that would be a better alternative than accepting she was the daughter of a psychotic criminal.

The sudden urge to talk to Uncle Nick overwhelmed Katie. "Turn around. We need to return to Starling and get Uncle Nick. And we need to call the police."

"If he's alive—"

Katie gaped. "What do you mean, *if*? You don't think those men..."

"Garrett will call as soon as he can," he finished.

The man was rambling. She steadied her voice using her best preschool teacher-to-student tone. "Who's Garrett? Your boss?"

"Deputy US Marshal Mason Garrett was your mother's handler. He posed as your uncle, Nick Romano."

The guy might be good-looking, but he was delusional. And armed. Great. *I'm stuck with a delusional, armed maniac.* "You think my uncle, Nick Romano—whom I've known my whole life, the guy who grew up in a foster home with my mother—is a US Marshal named Mason Garrett?" Katie shook her head. *Delusional.*

Silence filled the truck.

Katie considered the information against the things she knew for sure. Nick's ever-present weapon—blamed on his previous employment as a cop. Mama's final words—apologies that seemed out of place before her death—took on new meaning in the present moment. *I wanted to shield you. Someday I hope you'll forgive me.*

Katie had chalked up the confession to the massive amounts of painkillers flowing through her mother's dying body.

Too many pieces lined up, giving Daniel's words frightening plausibility.

"So, Nick—er—Mason Garrett was assigned to protect us from this Anthony Marino?"

"Yes." Daniel shot her a quick glance before returning his focus to the road. "This sounds like a bad mobster movie. But I assure you, those men weren't actors. You're in very real danger."

In danger from her own father. "Marino is a convicted crime lord?"

"Marino's business dealings include import and export of weapons and drugs. He's cutthroat and will do whatever it takes to get what he wants. If someone's in his way, he removes them."

Katie tilted her head. "As in, kills people?"

"That's an understatement. Killing is merciful compared to what Marino's men do."

"Quit with the cryptic talk." Irritation edged her voice.

"All right. Marino tortures people and murders entire families for revenge. He's ruthless."

Katie shook her head, wrapping her arms tightly around her torso. *God, I can't deal with this.*

Daniel reached for her, compassion evident in his eyes. "The truth—"

"Truth?" Katie snorted, anger rising above her reasoning. "Tell me, Daniel, was the loss of my mother, my closest friend, my deepest confidant, not enough? Why on earth would you think I could handle news like this right now?" She glared at him. The anger was misplaced, but she didn't care.

He blinked. "You said—"

"I haven't even eaten the casseroles friends and neighbors brought. I haven't cleared out her room. Did you know I gave up everything to move in with her when she was diagnosed with pancreatic cancer? Did you know that I've been caring for my mother full-time? I never minded. I love her. Would have done anything for her." Katie slapped the dashboard. "I want off this insanity ride. Take me home."

"I'm sorry. I can't do that."

The endless miles of fields, cows and highway blurred with Katie's frustrated tears but she refused to allow them to fall.

After what seemed like hours, she found her voice again. "What happens now?"

"First, I need to call my boss and update him.

Then, we get to the ranch. We're scheduled to fly to Maine first thing in the morning."

"Do I get an opinion?"

"Not if you want to live." Daniel pulled out his cell phone, swiped at the screen and made the call.

Katie scooted closer, intent on hearing his final declarations over her life. With her right hand, she fingered the oval object concealed in her pocket that Nick had given her at the house. She shifted in her seat, turning to face the window. Using Daniel's preoccupied moment to inspect the item, she surreptitiously withdrew it. A gold locket. Daniel's words had her shoving the item back into her pocket.

"Chief, Marino's men arrived sooner than we expected. Katie Tribani's with me. Garrett stayed behind to hold them off. Have you heard from him?"

She bit her lip. *Please, God, let him say Nick's okay.*

Daniel worked the steering wheel, gripping tight then relaxing his hold. Chief Bridges hadn't heard from Garrett. That told him everything he needed—and didn't really want—to know.

To her credit, Katie hadn't fallen apart. Impressive, but not surprising. Garrett said she was strong.

The transfer happened too quickly, but they'd expected that possibility. Months of training to take Garrett's place as her handler hadn't prepared Daniel for the way Katie would affect him. Her worry for Garrett's safety spoke of their closeness. Her willingness to go with him—a complete stranger—said she trusted Garrett. She'd placed herself into Daniel's care without huge resistance. Protectiveness he couldn't explain, beyond the job duties, pulsed through him. He barely knew her, yet months of studying her files bypassed his common sense.

Get a grip, Knight. Garrett had allowed his feelings for Evangelina to cloud his judgment. That would not happen to Daniel. No woman, no matter how gorgeous she was, would steer him away from being a marshal. He'd worked too hard. Sacrificed too much. Katie Tribani was under his protective duty. That's all.

A quick, stolen glance in Katie's direction whittled at his steadfastness. She hadn't even had a chance to grieve her mother's passing. Her black hair hung limply around her face, veiling her stunning emerald-green eyes. Modestly dressed, she sat with her legs curled under, leaning against the window. She was tiny—he'd guess five foot—no more than a hundred pounds and far more beautiful in person than any of the pictures he'd seen.

A delicate diamond cross hung from a thin silver chain around her neck. The jewels shimmered casting a kaleidoscope of colors inside the Suburban. Katie had grown too quiet. Maybe she was praying? She wasn't the only one.

Whatever the case, he was grateful for the reprieve of questions, though he knew there'd be more once she digested the information he'd been forced to provide.

Daniel checked the dashboard clock. They were close to the ranch and safety. At least until they could travel to the small airport in Grand Island. But the hours between destinations posed a huge vulnerability for them. Marino wouldn't give up.

"We've been driving forever. Where are we going?" Katie's inquiry interrupted his contemplation.

Daniel turned onto another dirt road. "The middle of nowhere. A little-used ranch owned by the Marshals' office."

The hum of the engine and crunching tires nearly drowned out Katie's murmured question. "Nick's dead…isn't he?"

He stared straight ahead. "We don't know for sure." But Daniel knew. Garrett wouldn't last as a prisoner. If he wasn't already dead, he would be soon.

"It's all my fault," Katie's voice quivered.

Daniel glanced in her direction and grimaced. He'd take a gun-toting criminal any day over a crying woman. "Don't do that to yourself. You deserved to know the truth. Garrett hoped your mother would tell you, but she asked him to do it after her passing."

Katie sighed. "When Nick doesn't want to do something, he's the biggest procrastinator."

"Yep." Daniel frowned. And that procrastination probably cost Garrett his life.

"I always thought my father was in the military and died in the Gulf War. There's so much I didn't question. I had no reason to. Mama never lied to me." Her laugh was laced with a bitter tone. "At least I didn't realize she was lying to me."

"Everything they did was to protect you." Daniel reached over to touch her arm, inadvertently grazing her leg. He quickly jerked back his hand and gripped the steering wheel, clearing his throat. "Their motives were good. The execution was a little off."

Why was contact with her causing him to behave like a crushing teenager?

He spotted the green mile marker at the last second, almost missing his next turn. Daniel yanked the wheel, dodging the large holes plaguing the minimum-maintenance road.

Katie grabbed the dash as the Suburban jostled over the unpaved route.

"We're almost to the ranch. Watch for a skinny lane."

She pointed to the left. "There?"

The road resembled more of a trail framed by tall, golden weeds that swished against the sides of the vehicle. The older ranch-style house sat several hundred feet away nestled behind a row of full oak trees. The bright colors of the autumn leaves danced boldly against the cerulean sky.

He parked at the end of the driveway, left the engine running and turned to face her. “Wait here. Let me clear the house. If I’m not back in five minutes or you hear anything, drive south and call Chief Bridges.” He tossed his cell phone to her, withdrawing his gun.

Katie sat taller in her seat and pivoted.

Probably gaining a better view of the road.

She turned, pressed her lips together and nodded. Her determination did little to mask the fear in her unblinking eyes.

Daniel tromped on the overgrown prickly weeds that consumed the vast yard. He made his way toward the back of the house. Sections of faded brown siding hung askew, half of the drain spout was missing and the sparse trim was peeling. *Hope the inside doesn’t look this bad.*

Only one point of entry besides the garage. Not good.

He returned to the front and peered at his black Suburban parked on the road. Cloudy remnants floated behind the vehicle, taking too long to settle and limiting his view. He craned his neck searching for any sign of Marino’s men.

Anxiety tempted him to ignore protocol, but he forced it down. Focus on the immediate. The dust provided a quick reveal for anyone driving along the road. Good advantage. He'd taken a ridiculous number of dirt roads and turns to ensure no one followed them.

Daniel returned to the attached two-car garage, entering the code on the keypad. The door groaned open. He inhaled a wave of dusty air and coughed, then covered his nose and mouth with the neck of his shirt.

The blue Dodge Ram sat inside. He checked the keys were in the ignition. Had Garrett remembered to fill the gas tank?

Gun poised, he climbed the small set of stairs leading to the house. The door gave an ominous creak as he pushed it open. Olive-green appliances and a yellow counter dated the adjoining kitchen. He moved through to the living room, sparsely furnished with an old-fashioned brown plaid couch and matching recliner. A coat closet near the front door stood ajar.

Daniel stepped to the side, fixated on the open space.

Movement? Or shadow?

He swallowed and aimed his gun at the closet.

"US Marshal, come out with your hands up."

Silence.

Daniel repeated the command.

The cuckoo clock on the wall ticked away seconds.

He reached forward, keeping a healthy distance,

threw open the door and jumped back. A pair of Carhartt overalls and coat swung in the otherwise empty space.

Daniel snickered. *Glad Katie didn't see me make a complete fool of myself.*

Refocused, he continued to the right, entering a short hallway. Two bedrooms located on the left side sat adjacent to the bathroom. Both included double beds, nightstands and small chests of drawers. The beds weren't made, but the mattresses appeared new, covered in clear plastic.

He moved into the first bedroom and flung open the closet door. The smell of mothballs filled his senses. He peered under the bed and spotted nothing, then walked into the second bedroom. Last, he cleared the small bathroom. The porcelain circa the early sixties in robin's-egg blue took up nearly all the movable space.

Daniel rushed back through the garage to the Suburban.

Relief was evident on Katie's face.

He gave her a reassuring smile.

"That was the longest five minutes of my life," she exhaled.

"Mine too," he quipped.

Katie's light chuckle made him grin. He slid behind the wheel and drove the Suburban into the garage beside the Ram.

"Whose truck is that?"

"Marshals Service. We need to change vehicles.

Marino's men know this one." He shut off the engine. "C'mon."

Daniel hit the garage door button and led Katie into the house. She pressed against his back.

"It smells funny," she whispered.

"Hasn't been used in a while."

The early afternoon sunlight streaming through the dusty windows provided plenty of illumination, but Daniel flipped on the kitchen light switch. "Two bedrooms and one bathroom. You get first pick." He pointed to the hallway. "Linens are in the closet."

Her dazed expression said the adrenaline rush had subsided. Katie plopped down on the bed of the first room she entered, rustling the plastic mattress cover.

He knelt in front of her. "I'll see what we have in the way of groceries. You hungry?"

She shook her head. Exhaustion apparent by the shadows around her half-lidded eyes. A stray section of her hair drooped over the left side of her face.

Without thinking, Daniel reached up and tucked it behind her ear, careful not to hit the silver hoop earring. *What possessed me to do that?*

"Mama's favorite pair." She touched the earring, drawing his attention to her slender neck.

Daniel stood and shoved his hands into his pockets. "Let's move to the kitchen. Maybe there's even something edible here not from 1970."

That earned him a laugh. He liked the sound.

"Garrett stocked the cupboards." Daniel rummaged through the cabinets, shuffling the canned vegetables and boxes of pasta, cereal and quick-fix meals.

"I'm not hungry."

He leaned against the counter cognizant of the space between them. "You need to keep up your strength."

Katie slid onto a chair at the table and put her head in her hands.

He moved to her side wanting to hold her, comfort her. Instead he touched her shoulder in an awkward I-care-but-I'm-keeping-this-professional pat.

"They had this secret life totally outside of my reality." She closed her eyes for a moment.

Daniel didn't speak. What could he say?

"I'm scared," she admitted.

"Of what?"

"I don't know." She pushed back from the table and stood. "This morning I didn't think anything could be worse than losing Mama. Now I'm running from my biological father and I've never even met him." Katie paced the rectangular kitchen then leaned against the old yellow Formica countertop. "Mama's life inspired so many. The congregation wanted to honor her with the newspaper tribute. When Uncle Nick—er, Garrett—ordered me not to send in her picture, I rebelled. Like usual. We've had a battle of the wills since I was a teenager. But then I got to feeling guilty and decided it wasn't worth arguing over, so I asked the editor not to print the picture, but I was too late. No wonder Nick was so furious with me."

Daniel dropped onto a seat. "He wasn't angry at you. He was angry at himself."

"Why?" Katie held his gaze.

"For keeping Evangelina's secret and not telling you the truth."

Katie returned to the table, sitting across from him. "If Marino wants to kidnap me as you say, why shoot at us?"

Good question. One he'd been tossing back and forth since they'd escaped the goons. "Honestly, I'm confused about the same thing. Marino would want you alive. It doesn't add up with what we believe."

And it meant they were possibly up against another enemy. The problem was…who?

THREE

"I need some air." Katie hurried to the front door and yanked it open. A fresh breeze met her, and she inhaled deeply. She skipped several of the cement steps and ran out to the gravel driveway. The reality of her surroundings barricaded her, an invisible prison wall.

There was no place to go, but she needed space...distance...an escape. Time to walk off the emotions flooding her in overwhelming waves. She walked laps between the driveway and house, frustration mounting with each forceful and fast-paced step.

She'd told Mama everything. Her deepest secrets, wishes and dreams. They'd been best friends. The one person she'd trusted more than anyone. Why hadn't Mama trusted her enough to tell her the truth? The sorrow was so heavy it pressed in, crushing Katie's heart.

The truth will set you free. The words she'd read in her morning devotional seemed cruel and ill-timed. Wasn't the truth made to shed light on the darkness? Katie didn't want to know the truth. It was anything but freeing. At the moment, it was stifling.

Debilitating.

Exhausting.

Katie circled the house for the second time.

The crunching of gravel behind her announced Daniel's presence.

Irritated and relieved, she bit out, "I don't want to talk."

"Okay." He moved to her side.

"I want to be alone."

"No can do." His refusal left no room for argument. "Don't blame you for being angry."

Her anger deflated, slowing Katie's pace. "I'm sorry. You didn't deserve my attitude. Thank you, for being honest with me. You're the only one who has been."

Daniel didn't answer, and his footsteps stopped.

Katie turned, following his gaze. A small cloud of dust trailed in the distance. He murmured under his breath.

"Maybe I should just go with them." Katie placed a hand on his shoulder. "How am I supposed to live a fabricated life that I didn't even know I was a part of? I'm done being a puppet for everyone. Contrary to popular belief, I do have a brain."

Daniel pulled his gun from the holster at his hip. "I appreciate your idea, but I'm asking you to trust me. You said you wanted to be able to make up your own mind. Let's get the facts, and you can do that. While you still have options."

Katie's emotions battled her instincts. She could end this ridiculous hunt. Face whatever or whoever was coming. Images of the men shooting at them interrupted her internal debate. She rocked back on her heels. She needed more facts. Daniel's input. He was the only connection to her past.

"I've been brutally honest with you concerning Marino." Daniel spun, jaw tight, and dragged her between the cover of the trees, his focus still on the approaching vehicle. "Remember what I told you about his methods."

A red four-door Honda turned onto the dirt road, kicking up dust and rocks. The tinted windows hid the passengers. The speed of the vehicle increased.

Her heart pounded.

"Katie." The urgency on Daniel's face momentarily persuaded her to follow him.

Bark splintered next to their heads.

He ducked, yanking her down next to him. "Negotiations are over. You can come willingly or I can carry you. Make a choice."

She didn't get a chance to respond. He grabbed her arm, dodging between the trees, and lunged toward the open front door of the house.

Glass shattered from the living room window.

Katie screamed, ripping free of Daniel's hold to cover her head with her arms.

"Head to the truck," he ordered.

Two men burst through the front doorway, wielding guns.

"Get them," the shorter of the two screeched.

"Go!" Daniel pushed Katie out the door to the

garage and pulled it closed behind them. He held tightly to the handle as the intruders banged and shouted on the other side. “Get in the Ram. Garage opener’s on the visor.”

Katie ran to the truck and climbed in. She started the engine, hit the garage door button, then turned to watch for Daniel.

The garage door groaned open. Light immersed the darkened space.

“Daniel, come on.”

He held the door handle, his boots braced on either side of the wooden frame. In the second he released his hold, the larger of the intruders lunged through, splintering the door. He tackled Daniel, and the two tumbled down the few steps onto the garage floor.

Daniel broke free from the entangled battle and aimed his gun.

Katie gasped.

The man swiped Daniel’s legs from under him, and she heard the clatter of his gun hit the ground.

Wild-eyed, Katie scanned the garage. Where had the other man gone?

As if sensing her question, Daniel turned to run.

The man sprinted in from the open garage door, aiming a gun at Daniel. He shot and missed as Daniel ducked behind the bed of the truck.

Katie sprawled on her side, searching under the seat for a weapon.

Nothing but dust.

She nearly fell out of the truck when the door opened and one of the assailants reached in. He grabbed her by the hair, dragging her from the vehicle, and shoved her against the driver's door.

The man was short and skinny, standing a little taller than Katie. He was ugly with black eyes that he narrowed at her. "Isabella, we're here to rescue you. Don't fight." His breath reeked of cigarette smoke.

Katie winced. Something was off.

The darkness in his eyes. The way he looked at her.

"I'm not Isabella. You've got the wrong person," she pleaded.

He grabbed her wrist, twisting. "You're the one."

"Let go. You're hurting me." Katie drove her elbow backward into his stomach.

He released his hold, and she turned to run. The man snagged her around the throat with his arm, pulling her against his bony chest.

Katie clutched the arm at her throat.

"Stop, before you make me mad," he seethed.

Nick's self-defense training bounced to the forefront of her mind. *Let him think he's won, then attack.* Katie relaxed her grip.

She felt the man step back slightly. "Good girl."

Katie thrust the back of her head into the assailant's face; the crack of bone and cartilage confirmed she'd hit her mark. He released his grasp and stumbled backward, falling against the garage wall. Katie's heart pounded in her ears.

The sound of screeching tires drew her attention. The third assailant fled the scene.

"He got away," Katie said, as Daniel ran toward her.

"Yeah, and he'll be back with more of Marino's cronies. Well done, by the way." He pointed to the man Katie had knocked out.

"Ditto." She rubbed her head. "That hurt more than I expected." She leaned back to see around the bed of the Ram. Both men lay on the ground.

"Is he dead?" Katie pointed to the man Daniel had fought.

"No, just unconscious. Let's get them both tied up before they come to or more return."

Daniel and Katie worked together, securing both men in the corner of the garage before closing the door.

"That should hold them." He tightened the last knot. "Let's get out of here. I'll call for backup on the way."

A few minutes later, they accelerated down the dirt road, and Daniel called for reinforcements.

"Now where?" Katie secured her seat belt, bounced on the cushion and gripped the armrest as the truck careened over the bumpy ground.

Either he was lost in thought or upset. Daniel's taut facial expression and his grip on the steering wheel illustrated an emotion Katie couldn't quite identify. He swiped his cell phone screen again.

"Who are you calling?"

He ignored her and spoke into the phone. "Chief. Marino's one step behind me."

Katie strained to hear, but the voice on the other end of the line was muffled.

"We're going to Colorado now. I'll need a car there… Affirmative." Daniel tossed his phone to the console. His end of the conversation was short and unrevealing.

"What's going on?"

He gave her a sideways glance. "We're not waiting. We've got to leave Nebraska."

"Colorado?" Katie looked out at the stretch of road. No traffic around them. Thankfully, no other shooting pursuits either.

"We're taking a detour before heading to Maine."

"Okay." Wasn't as if she could negotiate. Her head swam. "Daniel, please tell me everything you know about the Marinos."

"Your mother fled with you when you were a toddler. She left your brother, Giovanni, behind."

Before Katie could respond Daniel continued. "Giovanni followed in Anthony's despicable footsteps in case you're wondering if he's a nice guy."

How did one go from orphan to having a brother and father all in one day? "Why would she take me and not my brother?"

"Evangelina said the boy was older and deeply

devoted to Anthony. She feared he wouldn't go willingly and might give away your location if she forced him."

"The man back there called me Isabella."

"Your real name is Isabella Catarina Marino," Daniel said matter-of-factly.

"This is all surreal. Do you have any idea how bizarre it is to have a total stranger know more about my own life than I do?"

"I can only imagine."

Did Daniel's knowledge of the Marinos include anything about the locket that Nick had pressed into her hands before she left? He hadn't offered information, and she hadn't asked. His professional manner and proven protection thus far made him trustworthy. Didn't it? Hesitation tugged at her. No. Not yet.

An hour later, Daniel and Katie boarded the Marshals' small white plane. No fancy lettering graced the outside of the aircraft, just simple black letters and numbers that Katie assumed had more to do with identification rather than adornment.

They walked up the few small steps into the cabin. The brown interior was as nondescript as the exterior. Daniel must have sensed her scrutiny.

"Government equipment is bland as a rule—however, we do have a competent pilot." His lips curved upward in the hint of a smile.

"I'll take competent over decorative any day."

"Take your pick." Daniel pointed to the few seats separated by a narrow walkway.

Katie sat on the right side and secured her seat belt. She gripped the brown plastic armrest.

"Nervous?" He gestured toward her death grip.

"A little."

"It's a quick flight. We'll be up and down before you know it."

I sure hope so. Katie's head seemed glued to the back of the headrest. She swallowed and took a deep breath. Once more, she contemplated discussing the locket with Daniel. He'd given no indication that he knew she possessed it. She needed an ally and like it or not, he was the only option she had. He might be able to explain what the big deal was regarding the locket's secrecy.

One niggling question kept her silent. If Nick trusted Daniel, why whisper the instructions? His warning rang in her mind. *Hide it. No matter what happens, don't let anyone know you have it.* Anyone included Daniel.

Katie flinched at the light touch on her arm.

"Sorry, didn't mean to startle you," Daniel said.

"I was lost in thought."

"I can see that. Just wanted to tell you that you'll need to wear the headset otherwise you won't be able to hear me." He gestured toward the black set dangling above her seat.

Katie slipped the heavy gear over her ears.

"You'll need the microphone near your mouth."

Daniel reached over. The light scent of musk wafted to her as he rotated the small spongy piece, grazing her lips with his finger.

Frozen in the seat by the unintentional caress and the delicious smell, her heartbeat reverberated in her head.

If he noticed her reaction, it didn't show. Daniel sat back. "Can you hear me?"

Not over the pulse in my ears. "Yes, as clear as if you were sitting next to me." The engine roared to life, louder than she'd anticipated. "I can see why we need the headset." She adjusted her volume.

The plane motored along the runway, and Katie's grip returned to the armrest.

"Anxious?"

"No, what gave you that impression?" she joked.

"Instinct. Keep talking, it'll take your mind off being nervous." Daniel smiled. "Ever been to Colorado?"

Katie gazed at him through hooded lids. "You're kidding, right?"

Did she actually see him blush?

"Sorry, dumb question."

"I've heard it's beautiful."

Daniel nodded. "It is."

The plane ascended and Katie's stomach lurched.

He placed his hand over hers and gave a gentle squeeze. "Relax."

Gratitude for his reassurance morphed into warmth radiating through her. He removed his hand, oblivious to Katie's longing for more of his comfort.

"Have you had to fly often in your job?" The plane leveled, settling the butterflies in her stomach. Katie tried to release her death grip on the armrest, but her fingers wouldn't cooperate.

"A few times in relocating witnesses."

"How long do you stay with the person after you move them?" The question sounded more desperate than she'd intended.

"As long as the assignment requires."

Good answer. Her tension lessened and Katie released the armrest. "Are all the relocations to the same place?" She cringed. "Sorry, I guess you aren't allowed to tell me anything like that."

Daniel's expression spoke of compassion, not annoyance. "I can't give you details, but I can say they've all been different."

Relieved at his willingness to keep talking, Katie asked, "Any place tropical? Not that I mind Colorado and Maine, but I've never seen the ocean."

Daniel's bemused smile quieted her nervousness. "I think tropical locations are saved for the elite marshals. Mine tend to be more inland." He chuckled.

He wasn't the elite? Katie studied her traveling companion. She took in the strength of his jaw, allowing her gaze to travel down his neck and resting on the arm so close to hers. As far as she was concerned, she'd got the choice selection.

Wow, this day has had too many adrenaline spikes and dumps. Keep your brain in the game, not on your crazy emotions.

FOUR

The dull drumming behind Daniel's eyes threatened a ferocious headache. Adrenaline waned along with the plane's engine hum, luring him with the temptation of sleep. He sat up, rubbed the back of his neck and fought the exhaustion. *Stop acting like a rookie.* Previous assignments had required more than thirty-six hours of concentrated efforts, and he was dozing after sixteen.

He stared out the oval window as they soared through the azure sky between giant cotton ball clouds.

Daniel recalled Garrett's advice. "Never let yourself get too comfortable. Always remember your enemy is working against you. He's studied you. Knows you better than you know yourself."

The words referenced Marino, but they'd hit Daniel from a deeply seated place. Reminders of messages from his father's pulpit. Pastor Knight forever drilled into his children the need for a relationship with God. Something his sister, Brittany, hadn't wanted to pursue.

Daniel's parents agonized over years of Brittany's repeated drug use and finally her disappearance. Three stints of rehab and nothing changed. He'd held out hope that she'd be healed and return home, but reality was a heartless game changer.

Agitation rose and Daniel shifted in the small

seat, mentally shaking the thoughts of his sibling from his mind. He'd spent too much time worrying about Brittany. Katie needed his undivided attention not a focus split with his personal issues.

Daniel had worked hard, even been handpicked by Garrett to take his place. Meticulous training and grooming started with the review of Marino's massive file. That proved beneficial and chilling. Marino's criminal activity was so heinous, the Marshals used his case studies for the recruit procedural material. No assignment before threatened to be as dangerous.

He sighed. All that mental preparation barely touched today's experience, considering he'd never been shot at so many times in his entire career.

Daniel straightened his legs out and reached above his head, smacking the short ceiling as he stretched out his body's stiffness.

The case files were ingrained in his mind, giving him a false sense of knowing the Tribani women personally. Nothing equipped him for the way Katie ignited his senses. That was more of a rookie mistake than anything else. Falling for the petite brunette beauty was the last thing either of them needed. Besides, being romantically involved with a witness would be detrimental to his career. No woman, no matter how beautiful, was worth that.

Daniel's gaze drifted to where Katie slept in

her seat. This day must've been a nightmare for her. Other than the brief emotional outburst, she hadn't acted the way he'd expected. Instead of being a complete weeping mess, she'd given him anger and a quick walk around the not-so-safe-house.

He stifled a smile.

The sun shone on Katie's flawless skin, and her lashes fluttered. What was she dreaming about? Some part of him hoped it was him.

Knight, you need caffeine. Daniel rolled his neck, gripping the armrest of the Cessna.

The captain's voice crackled over the headset. "Prepare for descent."

"Affirmative," Daniel answered.

He waited as long as possible, not wanting to disturb Katie's serenity. As they taxied on the tarmac, Daniel gently touched her arm. "Katie."

Her eyes fluttered open. "Are we in Colorado?"

"Yep. Plane's landed."

She scooted back into her seat, peering out the window. "I thought the Denver airport was huge."

"We're at the Centennial Airport. Less busy. We'll travel by car the rest of the way." Daniel removed his headset and got out his cell phone. "Let me notify Chief Bridges of our status." He typed and sent the text, then unbelted from his seat. "How was your nap?"

Katie grinned. "Sorry, was I snoring?"

"You snore?"

"Like a freight train," she confessed with a laugh.

She had the kind of laugh that made him want to join in. Her green eyes sparkled, and her high cheekbones formed a model-worthy smile. She blinked, and Daniel realized he'd been staring at her.

"Let's get moving," he said a little too enthusiastically, leading her off the plane.

They trekked across the tarmac, and he searched for the requested vehicle. Right on cue, his phone pinged with a message from Chief Bridges. "We're looking for a Ford Taurus."

"There." Katie pointed to the white car parked near the hangar.

"I might have to start calling you Eagle Eye."

She rolled her eyes. "You mentioned Colorado as a detour to Maine?"

"Yes."

"I'm confused. Why not go straight there?"

"Gut feeling." Daniel held the door open for her. It wasn't entirely untrue. Maine was in the plan, but first, he needed to get to the top of the Manitou Incline.

He walked around to the driver's side and climbed in. The *Hawaii Five-0* theme song resonated from his cellphone.

"Cute." Katie smiled.

Daniel pulled out his phone and swiped to answer the call. "Chief, I just sent you a text."

Chief Bridges snorted. "I hate texting. Phones are made for talking, not typing."

Amused, Daniel grinned.

"Have you seen any sign of Marino's men?"

"No, sir."

"Good then it's time for me to remind you how this works."

Daniel braced himself for the berating to follow.

"When you called, I didn't question why you chose Colorado over my specific instructions to head to Maine."

"Thank you, sir. I took the initiative to make an executive decision—"

"Two problems with that, Knight. First, you're no executive. I approve locations, not you. Last time I checked, I'm in charge. Or were you promoted overnight? Did I miss the ceremony?" The chief's sarcasm bit through Daniel's waning confidence.

"No, sir." He rubbed the back of his neck and leaned against the headrest staring at the vehicle's fuzzy black ceiling.

Silence.

Bridges audibly sighed.

Daniel pictured Chief Bridges pacing his office. His short stature and booming voice were so contrasting that at times it was comical. In the

Marshals' office, no commander was more respected and trusted.

"I don't appreciate your execution—however, it was a smart move."

No way. Had Bridges complimented him? Daniel closed his gaping mouth.

The chief's volume decreased. "We got word from the Nebraska State Patrol. Garrett's body was found in the ashes of the Tribani home. He'd been shot. Several times. Looks like Marino's goons attempted to make him talk. The coroner's report hasn't come back yet. NSP stated the scene was gruesome."

Daniel swallowed hard, gripping the steering wheel with such force his hand cramped. He glanced at Katie then quickly averted his eyes. He couldn't bear to answer the questions in her expression.

The news wasn't surprising. It was the finality of knowing Garrett was dead that sucked the air from his lungs. Hope existed anonymously until it was ripped away.

Daniel opened his door and stepped out. He needed air.

"Daniel?" Katie whispered.

He leaned against the hood and heard her door open and close behind him. He'd have to tell her.

Her cautious approach and penetrating gaze made avoiding her impossible.

He gave a slight shake of his head and Katie returned to the car.

Bridges continued, "Stay away from Boulder. I believe you're compromised. I haven't figured out how. Don't tell me where you are. Make contact with me if and when you can."

"Got it."

"These men are vicious. Don't ever forget that. They'll do whatever it takes to find Katie Tribani. Are you able to keep her safe until I figure out where the leak is?"

"Affirmative."

"Good. And, Knight?"

"Sir?"

"Get out of Colorado ASAP and destroy whatever you're using to call me right now."

"Affirmative." Daniel disconnected and placed his phone on the pavement. Using the heel of his boot, he stomped the device into a pile of shattered glass and plastic. For good measure, he scooted the pieces under the back tire then slid back into the car, reversing out of the parking space. The device crunched under the tires as he drove from the airport.

Katie gawked at him. "Why'd you destroy your phone? Is everything okay? Was your boss angry?"

She'd watched his every move. At least she hadn't heard the conversation. Daniel's focus remained on the road. "It's under control."

He should've confessed to Bridges that he hadn't had a chance to grab the cash and extra weapon from the Nebraska safe house before Marino's goons showed up. In the end, it wouldn't change anything and one berating a day was plenty. Besides, he had Plan B, a.k.a Garrett's go-bag in Manitou Springs. They'd pick it up first thing the next morning and be on their way out of the state before lunchtime.

The phone call left him feeling better and worse, angrier at Marino and more aware than ever that he needed to protect Katie. Whatever the cost.

"I've always heard how beautiful Colorado is, but it's breathtaking in person. I've never been so close to real mountains. It's like having the psalms illustrated." Katie pressed her fingertips against the passenger window.

Daniel had remained quiet since the phone call and though she tried to engage him in conversation, he'd kept his replies to grunts. His change in demeanor was a good reminder that they weren't vacationing as a couple. He was protecting her, not courting her.

The sun rested atop the peaks and the multicolored sky painted a backdrop, giving the majestic formations a celestial quality.

"I can almost touch the sky."

In her periphery, Katie caught a hint of a smile on Daniel's attractive, grumpy face.

"That's wild." She pointed to a large flat-topped rock in the distance.

"Yep, that's how the town of Castle Rock got its name. They say that rock, or a butte, resembled a castle tower."

Finally, he speaks. She smiled. "Castle Rock. Cool name."

"It's a great place. When we've actually got time to check it out, I'll take you through and we'll have lunch or dinner. There are some excellent restaurants in town."

Her heart did a tiny happy leap. "I look forward to it."

"Marino shouldn't have any way of knowing where we are, but keep watch for anything out of the ordinary." Daniel's authoritative tone held the not-so-subtle reminder to focus on the task at hand.

Katie flipped on the radio and chose a Christian station. "Oh, TobyMac. He's one of my favorites."

She sang along, tapping her fingers with the beat. The song ended, and she turned down the volume. "I have a dumb question."

"Okay."

"Where are we going?"

Daniel worked his jaw. "We need to make a little detour."

"And that would be to where?"

"You'll see."

Great, we're back to grunting answers. Katie's

mind wandered as the beautiful view flew past her window.

Why would Anthony Marino want her dead? Was he really as evil as Daniel painted him? Everything she'd believed about the imaginary military father now replaced with images of a half man, half monster image. And if Anthony was a monster… *Lord, what does that make me?*

"Lost in thought?" Daniel asked.

A headache split the swarm of emotions overwhelming her. Katie pressed her lips tightly together, holding back the tears threatening to escape while rubbing her temples. She hoped Daniel saw the slight shake of her head since she didn't trust herself to speak.

Katie focused out the passenger window. Multitudes of questions fought for attention. There was no baseline from which to start processing because everything she'd ever known was grounded in lies.

Another song on the radio started and ended.

"I don't even know where to begin."

"You've been handed a lot." Daniel's sympathetic tone touched her. "I think you'll like Manitou Springs."

His quick change of topics gave her the excuse not to elaborate.

"You're finally willing to share my new destination?"

Based upon his pained expression, Katie's comment held more snark than she'd intended. "Is it another Marshal location?"

"No. Part of the reason I chose it."

Katie considered his words. Not sure if she was reassured or worried. "But aren't we safer sticking with law enforcement?"

"Marino's men are a step behind us. Chief agrees there's a leak in the office. Somehow, they've known our every move. I won't take that chance again."

His confident manner reminded her of Uncle Nick. Fond memories were squelched. Mason Garrett. She'd have to get used to calling him by his real name.

Daniel merged from the interstate to a side road where their ascent was surrounded by red rock formations. The ground held a deep rust color. Combined with the varying shades of gold, green and crimson from the autumn leaves, the landscape was a sea of rich colors.

He pulled onto a narrow single-lane paved road. "Are you hungry?"

Katie couldn't remember her last meal. "No, the car chase and plane ride left my stomach queasy."

"I'm starved. Until I'm sure we're under the radar, we'll have to grab some quick groceries to take back to the condo. Although, I'd prefer to go to one of my favorite places, Amanda's Fonda. They've got incredible Mexican food."

Katie liked the way Daniel made it sound as if

he'd be around for a while. *It isn't an invitation to date—he's doing his job.*

She scanned the scenic area. There was no grocery store. Not even a convenience store. As they crested the hill, she spotted a small gas station, tucked into a cleft and surrounded by trees. Its broken sign dangled by one chain. He wanted to stop there?

Daniel parked in front of the store's entrance, answering her question.

She followed his lead, exiting the car.

The bell over the door rang, alerting the clerk of their presence.

The round woman with dark skin and short black hair stood barely tall enough to see over the counter. She smiled widely at them. "Let me know if I can help you with anything."

"Thanks," Daniel said.

Katie smiled at her and surveyed the store's modest interior, surprised at its well-stocked shelves. The smell of pizza under a warmer awakened her appetite. She grabbed a bag of pretzels, cookies, two ginger ales and a slice of the pizza, setting the items on the counter next to Daniel's purchases. Several frozen burritos, a bottle of cola, prepackaged cupcakes and an unfamiliar container with Santiago's printed on top.

Daniel grinned. "Changed your mind?"

Katie shrugged. "It's a woman's prerogative."

He chuckled and, for the first time, she noticed

the dimple in his left cheek, giving him a youthful appearance. Her gaze shifted, and she caught the cashier's wink. Katie's neck warmed. Had she been that obvious?

Daniel paid for the groceries and the cashier gathered them into a sack, handing them to Katie. She quickly followed him out to the car.

He sipped on the cola and started the engine.

Katie opened a bottle of ginger ale, and the bubbles tickled her nose. The carbonation provided comfort for her stomach. The pizza's aroma wafted through the car, and warmed her lap through the small cardboard container.

"If you don't eat that pizza, I'm going to."

She gave him a wry smile and lifted the box closer to him. "I'll share."

"I'm only teasing. Can't eat it anyway."

"Why not? Does the Marshals' office have a rule against pizza?"

He shook his head. "Lactose intolerant."

Katie picked at the pepperoni, pulling up a slice. The melting mozzarella cheese made a long string of oozing deliciousness. "Oh, wow, that's gotta stink."

"Eh, you get used to it."

She popped the meat into her mouth. A groan of pleasure escaped her lips.

"You're killin' me," Daniel mumbled.

"Sorry, I'll quit being a brat." She nibbled at

the pizza, trying not to make any noise licking the grease and sauce from her fingers.

They drove through the town of Manitou Springs. A long line of shops bordered both sides of the two-lane Main Street. Katie strained to see the variety of stores as Daniel drove steadily along the road. Candy and art stores. Restaurants. The place was picturesque with the backdrop of mountainous red formations nestled in shades of green and brown, surrounded by a diverse spattering of bushes in every kind of green Katie could imagine. The rocky terrain rose behind the town, towering above them. The sky was painted in shifting shades of pinks and purples.

"I can't believe how lovely it is here," Katie whispered.

"I've seen a lot of places, but nothing compares to Colorado, in my opinion. There's so much to see and do."

She turned to face him. "You sound like a television announcer."

"I'll keep that option in mind if this job doesn't work out." He grinned.

Katie liked Daniel. Not Marshal Daniel, he was off-limits. But this Daniel was someone she'd like to get to know...once she stopped running for her life.

FIVE

Katie surveyed the small neighborhood with houses of varying shapes and sizes. No cookie-cutter building going on in this place. Every home was unique. Some were tiny, older and barely constituted a house. Others were grand in size, shape and modern design. The strange part was, the combination of homes worked.

A soft haze of light warned of the setting sun, but she could still see the artful landscaping around the contemporary-styled stucco home. Several short trees and flowering bushes covered the rocky ground taking the place of grass.

Daniel shut off the engine and removed the key. "Glad the place has been taken care of."

Katie scooted forward in her seat to get a better view. "Is this yours?"

"No. It belonged to Garrett first, but he sold it to my buddy in California about a year ago. I only have access to the basement condo." A far-off gaze flickered over Daniel's face and disappeared before Katie could ask any more questions. "Haven't been back in a long time."

He exited the car eliminating the possibility for further queries.

What made Daniel Knight? He knew a lot about her life, and she knew nothing about his. Had this place been a romantic getaway? Did he have a girlfriend? She rushed from the car as he vanished around the back side of the house.

Katie admired the valley below. The towers of salmon-colored rock and evergreens dotted the landscape. The road they'd driven snaked around the wide curves fading into the protective mountain.

She nearly tripped over Daniel, kneeling in front of a small flowering bush. He lifted the center of three decorative rocks, removed a key and replaced the fake one.

She snickered.

He twisted and gave her puzzled look. "What?"

"Seriously?"

"Hey, it works."

"What's that?" Katie pointed out toward the valley.

Daniel stood and followed her gaze. "What?"

"Those big red rocks."

"Garden of the Gods."

Katie quirked an eyebrow, focusing on the formations. "That name is almost sacrilegious."

"Another place I will have to take you sometime. It's an incredible natural park. For now, we'd better get inside." Daniel moved to the condo door and inserted the key.

She waited patiently behind him, taking in her surroundings. A porch swing hung from the balcony above, and the cement patio held several

Aztec-type pottery vases. The area begged for her to hang out with a great book and a cup of tea.

Katie followed Daniel into the open concept condo, pushing the door closed behind her and surveyed the room. An efficiency-size kitchen with an oblong dining table and two chairs was at the far end of the condo. Two bedrooms bordered the living area, where a brown leather sofa and love seat were positioned across from a built-in gas fireplace with stone mantel. A large picture window eliminated the underground feel.

Daniel closed the multicolored drapes. He flipped on the black iron lamp sitting on the metal-and-glass side table. A matching coffee table held three candles sized in a stair-step design and magazines were decoratively staggered with the titles visible.

Pale blue glass blocks against the opposite wall caught her eye. Katie entered the space where a stackable washer and dryer stood to the left. On the right, a double vanity sink stretched across the rectangular room. A door separated the toilet and spacious white stone shower.

The place was clean and furnished with a modern flair. She continued her tour and inspected the two bedrooms. Quaint, both had queen-size beds covered by white down comforters and decorative pillows in pale blues matching the glass blocks.

The condo was everything opposite of the

ranch where they'd almost stayed. Katie was silently grateful.

"I prefer the bedroom closest to the bathroom. The other room is practically brand new," Daniel said from the kitchen, where he unpacked their small bag of groceries.

"How long will we be here?" The snappy remark surprised Katie, and she looked down. Daniel had been nothing but protective and kind. "Sorry, I didn't mean to sound rude."

He placed items in the refrigerator and she was glad he couldn't see the mortification burning her face.

"No apologies. I get it. I think we're safe here. Only my California buddy knows I use this place."

Katie walked to the bookcase next to the window. An eclectic variety of leather-bound books filled the shelves along with decorative animals made of porcelain and stone, finishing the condo's masculine decor.

She dropped onto the sofa. Too bad the fireplace was gas and not wood burning. The comfort and crackle of kindling would create a peaceful setting. Everything about the place screamed romantic getaway.

Daniel must have caught her staring at the fireplace. He walked over. "I'll start a fire."

"No, you don't need to." The warm autumn air didn't warrant the necessity. Besides, she didn't want to encourage the imaginary ambiance.

"Let me know if you change your mind." Daniel yawned. He slid onto the love seat and rested his feet on the table, boots still on. He completed the pose by folding his arms behind his head.

Within minutes, loud rumbling snores emitted from him.

So much for romantic.

Katie rose and stepped to the bookshelf, selecting a worn red leather volume with no title on the spine. She flipped through the stained pages, wrinkling her nose at the book's exhale of stale leather and dust. Both reminded her of the old stuffy library in Starling.

By the dusty leather, she'd guess it was more decoration than literary interest. Did Daniel like to read? She'd have to ask him. She sat on the couch and studied the antique, early edition of the legendary *Treasure Island.*

Daniel's rhythmic snoring continued. The tall stranger who'd burst through her home and thrown her over his shoulder, all caveman-like, had changed her life. Though her body could finally relax, her mind wasn't cooperating.

Katie yielded to defeat after the hundredth time of trying to focus on the words. She grabbed a knitted afghan from the back of the sofa and draped it over Daniel, taking a minute to study him. His dark hair shaved close to his head gave no indication to the type. Was it curly or straight? Thick or thin? Stubble shadowed his face giving him a rustic look. His full lips were pursed and his dark eyelashes fluttered. What was he dreaming about?

She leaned closer. The scar on his cheek told a story and finished off the bad boy persona. Was it from a knife fight with a Russian mob? Or the result of his years in a gang in Los Angeles?

A grin crept across her face. She'd read too many crime novels.

Daniel's loud snort and exhale caused her to stifle a giggle. He was handsome, but not her type.

Katie grabbed the book from the coffee table and walked into the guest bedroom. She flipped on the nightstand lamp and kicked off her shoes, stretching out on the bed. One more adjustment to prop up the pillows and she settled into the softness.

She withdrew the oval gold locket and studied the delicate design tracing her finger along the engraved flowery vine and *E* in the center. What was so special that she couldn't tell anyone about the jewelry? She unfastened it and sucked in a breath at the pictures on each side of the locket. One of her as a baby. The other of Mama smiling back at her. Tears welled in her eyes. How could she be angry and still miss her mother so much at the same time?

"Lord, I hope you can make some sense out of this mess. And get me home."

Home. She didn't want to go back to Starling.

Did she? Before Mama got sick, she'd secretly dreamed of living by the ocean. Any ocean.

Katie was homeless and running from her own father and she wasn't sure she understood why. She sighed and rolled over on her side, allowing her eyes to close for a moment.

Katie jerked upright and cringed. The awkward sleeping position cramped her neck. She used one hand to push herself into a sitting position, then massaged her neck with the other.

Where was she?

Momentary panic, then recollection. The condo in Manitou. The lamp on the nightstand glowed brightly, and the book she'd attempted to read earlier pressed against her leg.

Katie slid off the bed. "Daniel?" She walked into the living area and surveyed the space.

Flames flickered in the gas fireplace but he no longer snored from the love seat. Where was he?

Alarm increased her pulse, and she struggled to swallow.

"Daniel?" Her voice squeaked an octave higher than normal.

She started toward the door as it swung open. Katie jumped back meeting Daniel.

A wave of cool evening air drifted into the room as he pushed the door shut and locked it.

"Hey, I thought I heard you calling. How was your nap?"

The brief episode of fear subsided and irritation took its place. "Where were you?"

Daniel lifted both hands in surrender. "I was on the porch swing when I heard you calling."

"Sorry, I thought..." Katie shuffled to the couch.

"What? That I'd leave you here alone?" The corners of his lips curled upward, and she caught a glimpse of the dimple on his cheek.

Katie gave him a sheepish grin. Had she insulted him?

"I'm glad you're awake. I'm starving."

She shrugged. "I'm a little hungry too." An understatement based on her stomach's grumbling.

"Good. I'll whip up dinner." Daniel walked into the kitchen and opened the refrigerator, removing several of the packages he'd purchased from the convenience store. He placed the items on the counter, whistling as he assembled their meal.

"What would you like to drink?" Katie joined him in the limited space.

"Water is fine." He microwaved frozen burritos on red dinner plates, then set them aside.

She maneuvered behind Daniel reaching for cups. He turned, bumping into her. His hand went to her lower back, steadying her in the confined space. The strength of his touch had Katie's stomach doing summersaults.

"Whoops, didn't mean to run you over." He grinned and shifted to the side.

Say something. But words eluded her. Katie busied herself filling their water glasses and placed them at the table. She leaned over the counter intrigued at Daniel's culinary talents. Never before had a man—besides Uncle Nick—done any cooking for her.

It was so…natural being with Daniel. For a brief second, she imagined them as a couple, making dinner together. A ridiculous thought. She didn't even know him.

He scooped contents from the Santiago's container into a bowl.

"What is that?" Katie wrinkled her nose. The thick orange substance had her questioning his judgement.

Daniel set the bowl in the microwave to warm. "Green chile. It'll make these frozen burritos edible."

She raised an eyebrow at him. "I've never had green chile."

"It's the gravy of Mexican food," Daniel continued. "Goes on anything. I got the mild because I wasn't sure if you'd like spicy."

"I love spicy foods. Mama turned up the heat on everything she made."

"It's better spicy but mild is just as good. Trust me."

"Uncle Nick said to never trust anybody who says *trust me*."

Daniel laughed. "If you hate it, I'll find something else to make you." The microwave chimed, and he poured the green chile over the burritos.

Mama always said to try everything once and if she didn't like it, she didn't have to finish it. In this case, she was hungry enough to try it, hate it and still eat it. Katie's voracious appetite momentarily waned at the memories. Her stomach's grumbling vetoed any hesitation.

Katie quickly slid into a chair at the table, keeping her back to Daniel. If her ears were as red as they felt, there was no way he'd miss her embarrassment.

"Sounds like you're hungrier than you thought." Daniel set the burrito masterpiece before her with his dimpled smile, sending a shiver through Katie.

She focused her attention on the questionable plate wafting delicious smells and assessed the best way to taste it without committing to the meal.

"Dig in."

"Okay, here goes." Katie cut a small piece of the burrito's corner and took a bite. The spices blended together tingling her tongue. "Mmmm. It's delicious."

Daniel beamed satisfaction. "I hate to say I told you so. No, I don't. Told you so. But leave room for dessert."

She grinned. "I'll never doubt you again. What's for dessert?" What else had he bought earlier? "Cupcakes?"

"Yep. They're delectable. I know great cuisine. Stick with me."

Katie laughed. "Like I have a choice." She took a larger bite.

"Touché. Nothing beats a captive audience."

She grinned and their eyes met, locking. Katie looked away, uncomfortable.

Their dinner conversation grew quiet, and only the sound of their forks against the plates filled the atmosphere.

Katie scraped the plate clean resisting the urge to lick the remaining sauce. "I didn't realize how hungry I was. I haven't had much of an appetite since Mama's funeral."

Daniel went into the kitchen, returning with one of the prepackaged cupcakes centered on a small plate. He set it before her. "The key to good food is presentation."

She grinned and took a bite. "You know it does taste better this way."

He bowed and sat down. "Thank you for not being one of those women who pretends she doesn't eat sweets then wolfs down an entire carton of ice cream when no one's looking."

"Are you kidding? Food and I have a wonderful relationship." Katie tilted her head and made a silly face, eliciting a chuckle from Daniel. "I haven't had one of these in forever. Used to walk to the corner store and get them when I was kid."

"Tell me about Starling."

"Not much to tell. Small town where everybody knows everybody. I mean, I guess they *think* they do." She frowned at the rising bitterness, folding her hands on the table.

Daniel touched her hand. "The fact that it took Marino over twenty years to find you says Garrett and Evangelina did a good job of protecting you."

She tried not to look at his hand, concentrating instead on his words. "I've been so focused on the deception, I hadn't thought about the struggles they faced. I bounce between feeling angry, to betrayed, to confused."

"You have every right to be." There was warmth in his brown eyes and his hand remained on hers. Strong. Protective.

Katie nodded, appreciative he didn't try to minimize the situation. "Is it unusual for a marshal to stay with the same witness so long?"

"Yes and no. Garrett cared for Evangelina to the degree that he threatened to quit if he wasn't allowed to be her sole handler. It could've resulted in a conflict of interest." Daniel pulled back his hand.

"Wow, that's devotion."

"Yep. No offense, but I think it was kind of crazy. He short-sided his career options. I don't know that I'd be willing to do something as extreme. Aside from God, my career's always been my priority."

"You want to be in charge someday?"

"Most definitely. I'd like to make Chief before I'm forty." Daniel's face appeared to brighten at the idea. "Ambitious, huh?"

"No, I think it's great that you have aspirations. Honestly, I've never thought much beyond being a preschool teacher." Katie scooted back in the chair, crossing her ankles.

"I'm sure the kids love you."

That dimple appeared again, and Katie's pulse did a quick surge. "They're great to be around. I enjoy the parents, too, although at times I feel like an old maid compared to some of them. And it's not like there are any viable dating options either." Why had she just confessed that? Didn't matter, if he'd studied her files he already knew she'd never been on a date before.

"An old maid at twenty-five? Hardly."

"Do you date a lot?" She did not just say that out loud. Katie's chest tightened and the urge to crawl under the table was overwhelming.

Daniel shook his head. "Nope. I don't really have time with my job. Besides not many women would understand me jetting off to mysterious locations for lengthy periods of time."

Had there been a woman who didn't understand? No, scratch that. She didn't want to know.

New topic. Any topic. "Did your dad work in law enforcement?"

Daniel pulled back his hand, crossing his arms over his chest. "No, I'm the first in our family."

"Do you have siblings?" His aversion to share made Katie want to know more. She wasn't letting him out of this conversation that easily.

"I have one sister. My mom stayed home to take care of us."

"What does your dad do?"

"He's a pastor."

That was surprising. "You're a pastor's kid?" Katie shook her head. "No way."

"Why is that so hard to believe?"

She giggled. "I guess I don't picture a pastor's kid being a gun-toting cop."

Daniel's grin said he wasn't offended. "My sister was much better at playing the part. At least until a few years ago."

"Why? What happened?" Katie bit her lip. "Sorry, I'm being nosy."

"It's okay. Brittany got involved with the wrong people and made choices that drove her away." Daniel's lips thinned. "Thanks to men like Marino pushing drugs on the street."

An awkward silence passed between them.

Katie slid her chair back and stood. "Thank you for dinner. It was delicious."

"My pleasure."

They worked together in comfortable quiet

washing the dinner dishes, then reclined in the living room.

"Wish I'd brought a change of clothes or my phone."

Daniel pushed off the couch. "Let me check the drawers. Sometimes my friend leaves clothes here. Maybe there's an old T-shirt you can borrow."

He returned seconds later with a sports T-shirt and a pair of basketball shorts.

"Thank you." She took the clothes and laid them next to her.

"We'll pick up some things for you tomorrow."

Katie pulled the afghan from the back of the couch over her shoulders. "You'll find I'm a fantastic bargain hunter. Frugal is my middle name."

"You're speaking my language, although you get a stipend for clothing. Fortunately for you, I'm not personally funding your wardrobe."

The words provided the important reminder that their relationship was professional.

"What else can you tell me about my life?" Katie pulled the afghan tighter.

"Garrett loved you like his own daughter. Evangelina wanted to give you the most normal life she could under the circumstances. She asked him to pose as your uncle Nick. They came up with a fake childhood story about meeting in a foster home to explain the lack of family on both sides and their obvious physical appearance differences."

Katie considered his words. Mama's jet-black hair and caramel-brown eyes compared to Garrett's light complexion and blue eyes. "Go on."

"Choosing his successor was important to Garrett. He'd been my mentor from the start of my career as a marshal, so he said I was his first choice. Over the past year, I've been groomed specifically to handle your case." Daniel paused. "When Evangelina was diagnosed terminal, Garrett decided to retire. He wanted to make the transition after you'd had a chance to grieve, but the time line was moved up when your location was compromised."

Katie appreciated Daniel's candidness. He was easy to be around, funny and thoughtful. His fit, muscular physique was obvious under the athletic shirt hugging his arms and chest. He clearly worked out a lot, but there was no arrogance or self-importance about his personality. In fact, he barely talked about himself. He wasn't ugly. Far from it. He had a rugged, intense appearance. Intimidating. Everything she shouldn't find attractive since she preferred blond, blue-eyed businessmen. Yet, something about him was alluring.

She needed sleep; her emotions were quirky.

He squinted at her. "What? Do I have something on my face?"

Katie dipped her chin. She'd been caught staring. Nice. Better go to bed before she said something stupid adding to her humiliation. "Sorry, I guess I'm more tired than I thought. Can we talk more tomorrow?" She feigned a yawn. "It's been a long day. Would you mind if I showered and went to bed?" Not waiting for an answer, Katie stood and folded the afghan then laid it on the couch.

"Sure. Let's plan to head out by five thirty."

"Head out where?"

"It'll be a surprise."

Katie grabbed the borrowed clothes, holding them close to her chest. "I think I've had enough of those to last a lifetime."

"A good surprise this time."

She sighed. "Thanks for everything. I owe you my life. Literally."

Daniel rose and shut off the fireplace. "Fun isn't done yet. Thank me when this is all over."

Would running from her psychotic father ever be over? Could Daniel possibly promise that?

SIX

Daniel glanced at the clock. He'd give Katie a few more minutes before disturbing her prayer time. He leaned to the right side of the couch, gazing at her through the partially opened bedroom door.

She sat on her bed with the worn old Bible she'd borrowed from his bookshelf. Her eyes were closed, and her lips moved ever so slightly though she made no sound. Guilt washed over him for invading the intimate moment.

Daniel stood and paced a circle around the living room, running his hands over his head. He had to get Garrett's emergency go-bag. *Please, Lord, let the bag still be buried at the top of the Manitou Incline.* Without the money, they'd be at the mercy of the Marshals' office and whatever leak would lead Marino's men to them.

How many ways could he mess up this detail?

Reservation about sharing the truth behind the needed trip today had him in the paralysis of analysis. He should tell Katie, but what difference would it make? Protection detail was his job, not hers.

Daniel pulled out his wallet and counted the remaining few dollar bills. They needed Garrett's go-bag. That meant making the trip to the Incline, regardless of the possible danger. The sooner they got moving, the better.

He spun on his heel and moved to the kitchen, pouring two cups of the freshly brewed coffee. Carrying the mugs, he walked to Katie's bedroom door.

As if sensing his presence, her eyes opened, and she turned to face him.

A swirl of steam floated above the warm liquid.

"Thank you." She took the cup from Daniel's outstretched hand.

"I hope I'm not interrupting." That wasn't entirely true.

"It's okay. I was finished."

"Didn't know if you'd want creamer."

Katie smiled. "I can do without. Uncle Nick, er, Garrett, said I drank melted ice cream cones, not coffee."

"Melted ice cream cones?" He leaned against the doorframe.

"That's what he calls fancy coffee. Caramel Macchiato is my favorite. But I'll drink any caffeine in an emergency." She took a sip and wrinkled her nose. "Nope, I lied. Still need creamer." She stood.

"You're up early." Daniel followed Katie into the kitchen.

"Didn't get much sleep."

"Sorry to hear that." Altitude sickness. Daniel inwardly cringed. He hadn't considered the possibility. Was that the reason she hadn't slept? "Uh, how are you feeling now?"

"I'm okay."

"Are you tired? Have a headache?"

She tilted her head. "No. Why?"

Daniel's shoulders relaxed. "I forgot to warn you about altitude sickness."

"I've never heard of such a thing."

"Happens to folks who aren't used to the high elevation. One symptom is trouble sleeping." He didn't add *And usually requires a day or two of rest.* They didn't have a day or two.

"I'm all right. The coffee's helping to revive me, and I needed the time this morning to pray and think."

"Any great revelations?" Daniel sipped his coffee.

Katie walked to the couch and sat. "Mama had to have good reason to leave Anthony, and I can even understand the reason she left behind Giovanni. I just hate being caught in this weird cat-and-mouse thing. I don't want to keep running, but Marino's men seem determined to kill me. I feel so helpless. What am I supposed to do?"

"I can help with that."

"Oh, yeah, how?"

"Up for a hike today?" His voice sounded a little too jovial to his own ears. Why not throw a cartwheel in too?

"Only if it means we forgo the car chases." She grinned. "Could we see the Garden of the Gods?"

Not today. But definitely another time. "Possibly. I want to take you someplace first."

"Sounds mysterious."

Daniel's gaze flitted to the partially opened curtains behind Katie. The early morning transitioning sky colors meant sunrise was quickly approaching. "We should get going."

Katie sighed. "I suppose."

Daniel grabbed the dark blue backpack he'd pulled out earlier and filled it with four disposable water bottles and a pair of binoculars. "You have to stay hydrated in Colorado. Helps prevent the altitude sickness."

"Okay. Are we both playing pack mule?"

"We can trade off carrying the pack." He frowned. "Come to think of it, drink some water before we go. You don't have a headache now, do you?"

"I'm fine," she assured.

"Let me know if you start feeling funky at all." *Not that it'll matter if we don't get on the road and soon.*

Ten minutes later, they drove into the Manitou Incline's nearly empty lot. A lone Jeep sat on the roadside. Die hard. It was early. Dedicated climbers weren't fazed by inclement weather or days of the week.

Daniel drove slowly and surveyed the area, confirming it was empty. Satisfied, he parked the car and unbuckled his seat belt. "Ready?"

He scanned once more, contemplating the hike. Maybe they should leave and keep moving. *Yeah, Knight, and how would you fund that little excursion without letting the Marshals' office know your location?* Just because Marino's men hadn't found them didn't mean they wouldn't.

"Shall we get on with this adventure?" Katie stepped out of the car and slipped on the backpack.

He wanted to show her something fun, and this exercise was more than entertainment; Garrett made him promise they'd do the trip. Besides the climb would build her confidence. They'd get the go-bag and be on their way out of Colorado before breakfast. Daniel applauded his self-talk and plastered on a smile. "Ready."

As they walked toward the base of the Incline, their feet crunched on the gravel road.

The sun was peaking over the horizon. A huge sphere of bright orange surrounded by pinks, purples and blues. Though the hour was still early, Daniel knew it was strange there were no other hikers. He shook off the uncertainty.

He gestured toward the mass of rock and wooden railroad ties nestled between the evergreens and bushes. "This is the Manitou Incline. When I first joined the Marshals, Garrett brought me here. He said if I could make the climb, I could do anything."

"I don't see how climbing is proof of capability."

"Do you trust me?"

Katie's pause said more than her words. "Yeah. I mean, I think so."

"I'll take that as a *yes*. This is one of the hardest hikes in Colorado. It's not for the weak."

"You sound like a character in an old Western." Katie giggled.

"Garrett made you watch those too?"

She nodded. "Every Saturday."

His smile wavered, and he turned away. The reality of Garrett's loss weighed on him. Studying the intense landscape, Daniel recalled the day he'd made this climb with his mentor. The most pivotal point in his career. He'd contacted Garrett and confessed he was quitting. Without trying to talk him out of it, Garrett requested they meet at the Incline for a final climb. Though his mentor rarely left Evangelina's side, he'd arranged a temporary detail for her with the purpose of joining Daniel.

Another glance at the steps that led upward, disappearing over the top of the mountain, and he second-guessed the decision. Would Katie be able to handle the exercise? She wasn't out of shape, but he might be asking too much. She stood close to him.

"Maybe this isn't a good idea." But how else would he retrieve the bag? He couldn't leave her unprotected.

"Are you saying I can't handle the hike?" Katie shifted the backpack on her shoulder. Her green eyes sparkled in the morning light. A sassy smirk replaced her furrowed brow. "Oh, I didn't think... Are *you* not able to handle it?"

"I beg your pardon?"

"I mean, you are...older than me."

Daniel smiled at her spunk. "By four years, but thanks for that boost to my ego. I think I can handle the exercise, but it'll be interesting if you feel that way afterward."

Katie took a stance with her hands on her hips. "The bottom doesn't look bad. Just a long stretch of flat steps. And it progressively rises so I'll have a chance to build up to the hard part."

He didn't want to discourage her. Initially, the Incline didn't look intimidating. Daniel adjusted his gun in the holster, pulling his T-shirt over to conceal the weapon. "Let's do this. Do you like to hike?" He kept small talk between them, hoping Katie wouldn't ask about the chief's phone call or Garrett.

She shrugged. "I lived in Nebraska. Not a lot of hiking opportunities in corn fields."

"Touché." He chuckled.

"I've done long walks—does that count?"

"Uh...sure."

The air was chilly but refreshing. He needed this diversion. Needed to not think about Garrett.

Daniel led the way, and they moved easily over the steps.

"This isn't what I expected."

"No? What'd you expect?" Daniel played along. Was she going to cave?

"Just to clarify, you want me to trot up this… giant ladder-step-cliff-like thing?"

Daniel forced down a smile. "That's a creative description. The steps are made up of over 2,700 railroad ties. Think of it as walking up a colossal set of stairs. It's only a mile." He didn't add, *It's a 2,000-foot climb in elevation.*

Katie paused and shook her head. "Please tell me you're kidding."

"Nope. I never joke about hiking. Like I said, it's not for the weak."

"I'm not weak, and I can do this. I'm not convinced why I'd want to." Katie jutted out a leg, hand on hip.

His lip curved upward at the aversion.

"If you make the climb, you'll see you can do anything. But if you can't, it's okay. No harm done."

"I can do it. If I want to."

"Okay, do you want to? I know it looks terrifying."

"It's not terrifying. It's strange."

"Once we reach the top and you see how far

you've come, you'll be amazed. We can turn back now. Forget this whole thing." Daniel jerked his jaw upward.

"Are you kidding? And let you think you bested me? No way." She pushed past him and continued upward.

Daniel followed behind Katie. Her quick ascent made him smile. Give it another few feet and she'd slow down for sure.

"This isn't so bad."

"You're doing great," he encouraged.

Spiky green plants and spatters of small yellow flowers lined the path. Trees framed the way making the two of them inconspicuous. Daniel was silently grateful for that. It also made it hard to see if anyone else approached and that left him uneasy. He knew better than to force Katie to move faster and the higher they climbed, the slower her pace.

She moved to the side and sat on a massive boulder. "I. Need. A. Break."

"Drink some water." Daniel pulled a water bottle out of the backpack then turned to assess their status.

"I hate to be. Pessimistic," she panted.

Daniel took a long swig of water. "Yeah, about what?"

Katie put her hands on her thighs and leaned forward, letting out a long exhale. "Some of those railroad ties don't look secure. Are you sure this is safe?"

"They're stronger than you think."

"If you say so." She rose, pulling on the backpack.

"I probably should've mentioned this earlier, but once we start, there's no turning back. The only way down is from the top."

"Because?"

"The angle makes it hard on the body and the spikes, loose blocks and uneven steps aren't conducive for descent."

"You're not scaring me. Let's finish this."

He grinned at her fortitude.

They continued upward. The foliage parted giving him a better view of the parking lot hundreds of feet below. Their vehicle was the only car. Was it a national no-hiking holiday he didn't know about?

His casual gaze was stopped short as a black four-door sedan pulled up behind the Taurus.

Two men in suits exited.

His lightheartedness vanished. *You've gotta be kidding.*

"Daniel, is that…?" She'd seen them too.

His name on her lips should have been sweet, but it carried her fears and worry.

Daniel searched the area around them, silently berating himself for being careless. He removed his Glock from the holster.

"What are we going to do?" Katie whispered though the men were too far away to hear her.

There was no way around.

They were on display. Nowhere to hide.

No way to run back down the Incline.

"It's a one-way trip. The bail out trail is a possibility, but not if Marino's men are waiting at the bottom. We'll be safer at the top." He turned and took in the sight of the remainder of the climb. They had to finish this. Up was their only hope.

Katie's face paled. "No. It's one thing to do it for fun. I can't run away from them uphill."

"Yes, you can. Look how far you've come." Daniel pointed down. "We're halfway there."

She gripped his arm. "I think I'm gonna be sick."

"No, you're not. We can finish this." Daniel stooped, holding her gaze. "There's no way they'll make it up the steps in suits and dress shoes. And we're almost to the top. We'll use the distance to buy some time."

Katie nodded. "I trust you."

Three words that sent the jackhammer in his chest into overdrive. It was one thing to make the climb, it was another to attempt to outrun men determined to kill them while hiking. Katie's faith in him bolstered his courage. No way could Marino's men make it up the Incline dressed like that. At least, he hoped they couldn't.

SEVEN

The thin mountain air stung Katie's lungs as she and Daniel continued their upward battle on the Incline. Where was the top?

Katie paused; her chest heaved with exertion and fear.

Daniel's hand rested on her back. "Don't stop. Just keep climbing."

"How close are they?"

"Doesn't matter. C'mon, you can do this."

But she needed to see. Needed to know how close the men were to catching up with them. Katie clutched the nearest railroad tie and twisted around. The sudden movement combined with the sight of the straight vertical drop caused her to sway off-balance. Daniel's strong presence moved in her line of sight.

"Focus upward."

Katie met his eyes, inhaled and gave a quick nod. In a steady motion, she turned and concentrated on the steps. The steep path necessitated more of a crawl than climb. *At least in this position, I won't fall off.*

Hand on the railroad tie, she hauled her protesting body upward. *Help me, Lord. One more step.* The words became a mental chant. *One more step.*

Time stood still; her heavy breathing coupled

with Daniel's were the only sounds except for their shoes against the railroad ties and gravel.

How far had they gone? Katie paused, gasping for oxygen, fingers clinging on the steps and knees digging into the unforgiving wood. She closed her eyes; the daunting task weighed heavily on her resolve. "I can't keep going. I can't breathe."

"Don't stop, Katie. Slow is still progress." Daniel didn't touch her this time, but his words wrapped around her.

I'm going to die up here. And nobody will find my body because nobody will be crazy enough to make this ridiculous climb.

Had she said the words out loud?

No. She could barely breathe, much less voice her complaint. Her thoughts were magnified and Daniel's silence didn't help.

Her legs and arms shook with exertion.

"Katie, dig deep. Don't give up—you can do this," Daniel urged.

She was holding him back. He could easily make the climb but he was stuck going at her snail's pace. *God, help me.*

"How long will you cling up there before you realize there's no escape?" one of the men taunted from below.

"Come down and we won't hurt you," the other called.

Despite Daniel's encouragement and her own

fears, Katie turned. The men were slowly pursuing. One aimed a gun at them.

Daniel's hand again secured her. "Don't respond. Get closer to the ground."

She obeyed.

A muffled *pffft* and spray of dirt inches from her hand had Katie jerking back her arm.

"They're seriously shooting at us?" she rasped.

Daniel held tight, pressing his body against her back. She could feel the heaviness of his breathing. The warmth of his body. The smell of earth and soap. He was literally shielding her body with his.

"Keep down." Daniel returned fire.

"Lord, help us!" She twisted beneath Daniel's arched body and watched as the taller of the two men ducked and slipped, sending both tumbling backward.

Katie gasped.

They landed in a heap at the bottom. A tangled mess of dress suits and irritated assailants. One of the men had a broken leg, twisted in an awkward angle.

"Go," Daniel pressed, moving aside so she could continue the climb.

Katie pushed on. Deliberately and painfully making her trek up the mountain, her breath shallow.

"Are they coming?" she panted.

"No."

Daniel and Katie increased their pace.

If possible, the air was thinner. How did people in Colorado breathe? The railroad ties disappeared over the top of the mountain.

"We're almost there." Katie was excited for the first time at the sight of the end so near. The possibility of finishing propelled her forward.

"That's the false summit."

Katie blinked, forcing down tears of frustration.

As if sensing her defeat, Daniel added, "But we're close."

She contemplated throwing a temper tantrum but dared not use her already limited oxygen supply.

"Don't let it discourage you," Daniel said. "The men are leaving. Let's finish this."

His words helped, but each step weighed more than the last. Each one harder to make.

Katie paused, feeling every thump of her pounding heart and the fire in her lungs. *God, help me finish this.*

The sunshine beamed down, warming her. Like a shot of adrenaline, she took in the sight of the remaining climb and with a deep exhale, summoned the last bit of energy.

She stumbled over the last railroad tie to several cement steps encased with sand. Evergreens and other sparse trees and bushes decorated the peak. Light-beige-colored gravel was scattered around the cement steps. Two huge boulders centered the peak. Katie stood tall, gaping at the mountain paradise. Breathtaking. And she was alive.

She took heavy, sloppy steps to the center of the peak and collapsed onto the sandy area. The cool ground refreshed her sweaty body. Katie rolled onto her back staring up at the blue cloudless sky.

Daniel dropped next to her, wrapping his muscular arms around his knees. "How do you feel?"

Katie turned to look at him. His dark eyes met hers.

The gaze lasted longer than it should've, but looking away involved effort and Katie's heavy panting hadn't yet ceased.

She pulled herself to a sitting position, mimicking his posture and swiped at the sweat clinging to her back. Katie held her ponytail up higher as a cool breeze blew on her neck. "Be glad you don't have to deal with hair."

He laughed. "I'll give you extra points for that."

The man didn't look fatigued at all. "How are you not dying right now?"

"Years of experience? Besides, you're a flatlander." He gave her a teasing one-finger poke in the arm.

His touch sent shivers through her body.

"Whatever." Katie inhaled and succumbed to a coughing fit.

"Stand up."

She glared at him, still battling the racking cough. Daniel put his arms under hers and lifted

Katie to a standing position. He held her arms above her head. "It'll help you breathe."

The coughing subsided and she inhaled deeply. "Much better. Thank you." She peered down the mile of railroad ties.

Daunting.

Terrifying.

And she'd done it.

"I don't see the men."

Daniel stepped to Katie's side, placed his hand on her shoulder and followed her gaze down the steps. "I'm sure they found a way to get out of here. They've gone. For now."

She forced her thoughts back to the topic and not the fluttering in her stomach. "What if they're waiting for us below?"

"I have a feeling their little trip down left them too sore to do much. One had a broken leg for sure."

"No ambulance?"

"They won't draw any unnecessary attention."

"Might be hard to explain themselves."

Daniel nodded. "Exactly."

Katie inhaled deeply.

Exhilarated.

Thrilled.

"Then I can celebrate my accomplishment." She turned to face Daniel.

"*Your* accomplishment?" He smiled.

"*Our* accomplishment. Even though I practically had to drag you up the mountain," she teased. Katie danced around him, chanting, "We did it. We did it."

She hugged him full on. The strength of his arms wrapped around her triggered warmth that radiated throughout her body. Her laughter subsided. She wanted to pull back, create distance. The elation of the climb combined with the danger of the men, and Daniel's hands around her lower back awakened every nerve ending.

Their eyes met and his gaze drifted over her. Katie followed the contour of his jaw to his lips… inches from hers. She lifted her chin, bringing her face nearer in proximity, closing her eyes. Close enough for him to reach her. Willing him to kiss her.

He released his hold and stepped back. "I knew you could do it. Even without our motivating friends down there."

Katie's eyes flew open and she cleared her throat, wiping her sweaty hands on her pant legs. The heat on her face tangled with embarrassment and longing. "Right. Well, thanks for staying behind me. You could've made the climb and hung out here having lunch until I finished." Her nervous laugh came out a snort making the awkwardness worse.

"No way—it's all about the team work." Daniel cleared his throat. "Katie, I have a confession to make."

"Okay."

"I had another reason for us to make this climb. Garrett left me a go-bag buried over there." Daniel pointed to an evergreen tree.

"I don't understand. How did he know we'd be up here?" Katie tilted her head.

"This was Garrett's favorite retreat location. He said if anything went wrong, he'd leave me a fail-safe. At the ranch, I neglected to grab the money and extra weapon before we left. Wouldn't have been a big deal if we'd made it to Boulder yesterday." Daniel shifted from one foot to the other. "Chief Bridges said we're compromised. There's a leak in the office. He ordered me to stay off the grid. That go-bag is essential."

Katie turned toward the area Daniel had indicated. Garrett was always a step ahead, still taking care of her even when he wasn't there. A peace settled on her, although she didn't try to hide her disappointment at Daniel's information omission. The wounded expression on his face kept her from pressing too much about the issue. "You should've told me the truth."

"Duly noted." He gave her a slight smile, lifted the backpack and pulled out the binoculars. "Let me do some recon, make sure Marino's men are gone. Rest over there, away from the edge. Sip on a bottle of water so you don't get sick. I'll be right back."

Daniel walked to the back side of the peak closing the discussion. His absence, though only a few feet away, left her cold.

Katie obeyed his instructions, and watched from her perch on a boulder. Daniel surveyed the area through his binoculars and then moved to the evergreen he'd indicated. He lifted a rock the size of a basketball and dug the earth beneath. Within seconds, he produced a small red bag.

Why hadn't he kissed her? *Because he's on the job, not a date.* Katie couldn't take her eyes off him. His muscles were taut beneath the athletic T-shirt he wore. Her ears warmed. *What was she doing?*

Katie looked down at her own jeans and hoodie, remembering his rebuff. He wasn't interested in her and she wasn't interested in him. The idea of a kiss was merely an emotional response from the excitement of finishing the climb.

She turned her back to Daniel and reached into her pocket and withdrew the locket. For the most part, Daniel had been honest with her. Maybe it was time for her to get honest with him. The locket weighed with everything she dreaded and longed to understand.

"The only way down from here is the Barr Trail."

Katie spun, clutching the necklace. "You startled me."

"Gearing up to slug me for not telling you about the go-bag?" He nodded at her hand.

"No. I have a confession of my own and there's something I need to ask you about." Katie gave Daniel a brief explanation of how she'd come to own the locket. "I don't understand what the big deal is. There are pictures inside. I hardly think that it's a threat to National Security."

"May I see it?"

Katie dropped the necklace into his outstretched palm.

Daniel inspected the locket carefully and his brows furrowed. "I wonder..." He plucked out the pictures with his fingernail, and inspected the piece. "There are a series of numbers engraved."

"What?" Katie leaned over his arm. "Where?"

Daniel pointed to the inscription.

She gasped. "What are the numbers for?"

"I have no idea, but it adds credence to Garrett's warning to keep the necklace a secret." Katie didn't miss the tinge of sharpness in Daniel's tone.

Was Daniel angry that Garrett had kept the locket a secret?

His expression softened. "Katie, should I hold on to it for you?"

She considered the offer, then shook her head. "I appreciate the offer, but I'm not willing to let go of it just yet. However, I'd appreciate your help in figuring out what the inscription means. Once we're back to civilization."

He grinned. "I love a good mystery."

"Thanks." She secured the pictures inside and

slid the necklace back into her pocket. Somehow sharing the secret lightened her emotional load, even though she'd gone against Garrett's wishes. "You said we have to go down a different trail? As in, we don't have to climb back down those railroad ties?"

"Nope. The men are gone but I'm sure they'll be back. The trail is the fastest way…the only way down." Daniel gestured toward an opening framed by evergreen trees.

Katie gave a little dance of joy and fist pump in the air. "Yes."

Daniel chuckled. "You're crazy, woman."

"Right?" Katie rushed to him, planted a quick kiss on his cheek, grabbed the backpack and moved into the trail's tree cover.

Daniel's cheek burned from Katie's impromptu kiss. Not a kiss. A peck on the cheek. It didn't mean anything.

He forced his feet to cooperate, catching her before she entered the trailhead. "Hey, I'm leading here."

"As if I couldn't?" She turned and smiled.

Wow, she was stunning, naturally beautiful. No makeup or fancy hairstyle. Her long dark brown hair pulled back in a ponytail accentuated her face, drawing attention to those gorgeous green eyes the color of emeralds.

"I assume we're going down the mountain," Katie said.

Daniel rubbed the back of his neck. "Humor me."

She stopped and made a grand hand gesture letting him take the lead.

"Thank you." *Focus, Knight.* He'd come way too close to acting on his desire to kiss her. The thought sent heat that had nothing to do with the sunshine bursting through him. He knew better than to fall into transferred affection, especially in emotional situations like Katie's. Poor woman had just lost her mom and Garrett; of course she was confused. He was not. Whatever the case, they weren't here for romance. He had no intention of allowing anything inappropriate to occur between them. Commitment and long-term relationships did not mix well with his job.

The last thing Katie needed was some lovesick moron who was too goo-goo eyed to notice Marino's men. His foolishness nearly cost them their lives. If the assailants had been in better shape, adequately clothed or capable of making the climb, they'd be dead. So why hadn't the goons tried coming up the Barr Trail? Dad would've called it a gift from God. Daniel called it criminal stupidity.

Either way, he couldn't afford that kind of mistake again. And falling for the woman he was protecting was the worst thing he could do. They could be friends. She was fun and sweet and…

beautiful. He willed himself to monitor the area, grateful Katie couldn't see the boyish smile still stretched across his face.

The dry earth crunched beneath their feet. Birds chirped and the sun was warm against his skin. Really? He was giddy.

"Dumb question. Why didn't we go up this way?"

"What fun would that have been?"

"I need to read the fine print next time."

"Autumn is the best time to hike. The colors are outstanding," Daniel blurted. Great, now he sounded like a tour guide. Scenery was a safe topic.

"It's truly an amazing place. Daniel, check out this stump."

He stopped and turned.

Katie pointed to a dead tree stump. "It looks like a baby bear."

He peered closer.

"God does great work." She touched the wood, tracing the lines.

Daniel couldn't help but notice the deep evergreen trees surrounded by bush leaves in rusts and corals. Colorado was home. He'd never been anywhere that touched his soul like this place did. Would he ever be able to return here? If he accompanied Katie to Maine, he'd be forced to live there. Forced might not be the right word.

An uneasiness gave him pause. He surveyed

the area around them, listening for any sounds of unwanted visitors. A rustling in the trees had him stepping around Katie. “Shh.” He motioned for the backpack.

Katie handed him the bag. He withdrew the binoculars, spotting nothing more than the occasional squirrel or bird.

“Is something wrong?” she whispered.

Daniel pulled the strap of the binoculars over his head. Better keep them close, just in case. “Let’s pick up our pace—we need to get out of here before Marino’s men return.”

They increased their stride to a faster walk. He didn’t want to frighten her, but they’d been in the same place a little too long.

“Hey, I can see the bottom. That was a whole lot easier than the way up.”

“Our car is—” A sharp stinging in Daniel’s back halted him.

Katie was already on the ground.

He reached behind, and grabbed hold of a thin object, pulling it out of his lower back.

Tranquilizer dart.

He fought to stay awake. His vision blurred. His mouth went dry.

Daniel stumbled, grasping at the trees. He clutched a branch and struggled to right himself. He dropped to his knees and grabbed Katie, pulling her to him. She was too heavy and he couldn’t hold on to her anymore. No, he couldn't fail her now. He couldn't lose her.

He collapsed to the ground and the day faded into night.

The ground moved. Daniel fought the effects of the tranquilizer chemicals oozing through his system. How long had he been out?

He strained to open his eyes, listening to the purring of an engine in the distance. A truck? Two distinct male voices. Daniel struggled to focus.

He dragged his arm across his body, reaching for his gun. His coordination was clumsy, and it took him a minute to find his holster. The gun was gone. The effort was harder than he expected and his hand fell limply at his side.

Garrett would be so proud.

Daniel forced his eyes open. Darkness. His breath was warm and close to his skin. Something covered his face. He reached up, clawing at the fabric tied around his face and neck.

"He's waking up," a man's thickly accented voice advised.

"Not for long," another answered.

A slam into his nose sent shooting pain up Daniel's face. He licked at the warm trickle sliding into his mouth. Blood.

Before he could move, he winced at a pinch in his neck.

His eyes grew heavy.

"Is he out?" the first man asked.

"Give him another dose," the second assailant replied.

"No," Daniel protested, not sure if the words made it past his lips.

Another pinch and he fell back into the darkness again.

EIGHT

The hum of an engine mercilessly dragged Katie from a sweet dream of sipping lattes on the patio with her mother. The ground shifted slightly and she turned her head, allowing her eyes to flutter open. The heavy throbbing behind her lids forced them closed. Her body fought a silent tug-of-war between waking and succumbing to the sleepiness.

Katie squeezed her eyes tightly and tried again, fighting the drum procession in her brain. Her ears were plugged as if she were underwater.

Sunlight beamed through a small window, casting shadows on the confined quarters. Alarm coursed through her. She was on an airplane.

Daniel. Where was Daniel?

How long had she been like this?

Katie blinked to clear her blurred vision and attempted to scoot upright. The restriction of her limbs amplified her anxiety.

She jerked her arms, and the resulting clank of metal had her tilting to investigate. Each of her wrists was shackled on either side of the seat by handcuffs.

Separated by a dark wooden table, Daniel sat across from her with his head slumped down, face to his chest, unconscious. Both sat in white leather chairs resembling recliners. Based on his arm positioning, he was also handcuffed.

Lord, thank you that Daniel's here. Probably selfish, but she needed him.

Cherrywood encompassed the interior and the plush maroon carpet gave the space the appearance of a narrow living room, except for the rounded ceiling with little air vents. She leaned over her seat and looked out the window. Clouds and a brilliant blue background confirmed what she already knew.

The aircraft was much larger than the one they'd traveled in from Nebraska to Colorado. Luxurious. Definitely not government. Anthony Marino's?

Her pulse increased and her chest tightened. If he'd wanted her dead, she would be, right? Instead, she was on a plane. Something didn't compute. Why spend all that time trying to kill her only to abduct her? And why bring Daniel?

She craned her neck, confirming they were alone in the cabin.

"Daniel," she croaked. Clearing her throat, she tried again. "Daniel."

Katie stretched her leg under the table and kicked his foot. He didn't move.

She pushed herself upright. Were cameras watching her?

Two crystal decanters of what looked like water on the bar at the far end of the plane's cabin awakened Katie's thirst. She licked her lips, conscious of the dryness in her mouth.

The drum procession in her head returned. Katie combatted the beat by trying to remember how she'd gotten here. The last she recalled, they were at the Manitou Incline. She rubbed her neck. What had she been shot with? Something that knocked her out. But at least she wasn't dead.

Lord, please help us. Her imagination played on the possibilities awaiting them. Panicked, she tugged at the restraints. Her gaze returned to Daniel. His chest moved. *Good, he's alive.*

"Daniel," Katie called, not caring if anyone heard her. She stretched her leg beneath the table and kicked as hard as she could.

Daniel came to life instantly like he'd been cattle prodded. He jerked upright, his eyes wild as he looked around, settling his gaze on her. "Are you okay?"

Katie gasped; indignation filled her at the sight of Daniel's black eye and the crimson stream that had dried above his swollen nose. "Oh, Daniel. I'm so sorry."

He winced. "Do I look that bad?"

"Um, yeah."

"I'm sure it's uglier than it feels." Daniel wrenched against the handcuffs.

The cockpit door opened. A man in his forties with gray streaks in his hair and neatly trimmed beard exited. Dressed in a white turtleneck sweater and brown sports jacket, he looked like a college professor. "Ah, I see the two sleeping beauties are finally awake," he said, with the hint of an English accent.

He moved toward them, keeping a safe distance from Daniel. "Mr. Knight, please remember, we're at 30,000 feet. I'd hate for you to go skydiving without a parachute." He laughed a little too hard at his own joke.

"This isn't funny," Katie retorted.

Daniel glared at the stranger and he sobered.

"Depends on your perspective I suppose. I would have killed you after what you did at that quaint hiking place."

"Looks to me like you took the coward's way and attacked a restrained man," Katie said.

"Katie," Daniel warned.

"I didn't do that to your boyfriend." The man pointed to Daniel. "Although I'm sorry I missed the opportunity. By the way, Jack isn't thrilled with his new cast."

"You all tried to shoot us," Katie belted.

"Jack would disagree. Of course, he's not as rational as I am. I warned him and Greg not to try that atrocious climb, but they're both too pigheaded. I watched from the car and between the three of us, I must admit, it was funny to see them topple off. Like two overgrown Humpty Dumpties." He chortled. "Fortunately, for you, they're still recovering so they weren't able to join us on this trip. Besides, Mr. Marino wants you both delivered alive."

"Really? Why'd they keep trying to kill us? Seems to me, that goes against the 'delivered alive' strategy," Daniel challenged.

The stranger moved to the bar area at the back of the cabin. "Let's just say there were conflicting directions." The clinking of ice cubes into a glass reminded Katie of her own thirst.

"Could we get some water?" she asked.

He turned, acknowledging her. His leering glance sent an involuntary shiver up Katie's back. After several seconds, and two more sips, he set his glass down.

The man opened the mini fridge, withdrew a bottle of water and walked toward them.

"First, give the water to Daniel," she insisted.

The man ignored her, twisting off the lid, and tilted the bottle into her mouth. She gulped greedily. The assistance left her feeling like a toddler with dribbling water on her chin. "Can you please remove the handcuffs?"

He guffawed and set the bottle on the table. "I'm not crazy. Your boyfriend here would talk you into attempting an escape." Using a napkin from the bar, he gently dabbed at her face and chin, lingering longer than necessary on her neck.

She flinched and shrank back into the seat.

His dark eyes flashed.

"I'm sure Mr. Marino would love to know how you mishandled his daughter," Daniel interjected.

The man's jaw tightened and he returned to the cockpit, slamming the door.

"Thank you." Katie ducked her chin, wiping it on her shirt.

"I would've preferred to punch him," Daniel growled.

"Was it me, or did he look like a college professor?" she whispered.

The corner of Daniel's lip lifted slightly. "I like that, we'll call him The Professor."

"Where are they taking us?"

"Marino's got several houses. Could be any one of them." Daniel shifted in his seat.

"Florida," the man answered over the speaker.

Daniel gave a sideways glance toward the ceiling. "Guess that answers whether we're being watched," he murmured.

Katie tried again to work on the kidnapper's humanity. "Would you please remove my handcuffs? It's not like we can go anywhere. They're hurting my arms."

"You'll live," the voice responded over the speaker. "Be quiet and enjoy the ride or I'll be forced to add a gag to your accommodations."

Katie clamped her mouth shut.

"The good news is, if they wanted us dead, we'd already be dead," Daniel said.

"I guess. I'm sorry you're in the middle of this

mess. I know I acted like a two-year-old when you told me about Anthony being my father and all." Katie didn't meet his eyes. *Sorry for kissing your cheek and making a fool of myself dancing on the top of the Incline.* She wasn't going to remind him. If he didn't bring it up, neither would she.

"You had every right to."

"Maybe, but I shouldn't have taken my anger out on you. You didn't deserve that." Katie let out a long exhale.

Where was the backpack? She leaned closer to Daniel. The faint smell of earthiness from their hike drifted to her.

She searched around her legs. "I don't see my backpack."

"That's because I have it," the voice on the speaker answered.

"Can I have it back?" Katie asked.

Silence.

"Daniel?"

He met her gaze but didn't say anything.

"I'm scared."

"Like I said, if he wanted us dead, we would be."

The sound of the plane's engine created background noise filling the small, quiet space. After several long minutes, Daniel spoke. "I had it all figured out, ya know?"

Should she respond? She didn't.

"Garrett spent twenty-plus years without having to outrun Marino at every turn. I thought I could do the same." He sighed, and she watched as his Adam's apple bobbed. "I underestimated him."

"Did Marino ever come close to finding us?" Katie wondered aloud.

"Not really. His efforts increased tenfold when he was released. He had some pretty hefty charges. Garrett never mentioned him getting wind of your location."

"What're they going to do with us?"

"I suspect we'll get to Marino's home. He'll find a way to get rid of me. But I won't make that easy for him. He'll try to manipulate you." Daniel met her eyes. "Katie, you need to remember that no matter how charming or terrifying the guy might be, every word out of his mouth is a lie."

"Now, now, that's no way to talk about the man who holds your life in his hands," the stranger spoke over the speaker.

Katie's heart drummed in her chest.

"Get ready to land," the man advised over the speaker.

The descent was quick. As they touched down, the velocity pushed Katie back into the seat. The wheels growled as they slowed and taxied. She'd flown more in twenty-four hours than she had her entire life.

Katie turned to Daniel. He shook his head, indicating he didn't want attention drawn to him.

"Don't get yourself killed," she warned, concentrating on the cockpit door.

The plane stopped, and The Professor—as she deemed the man—returned, gun in hand.

"I hope you enjoyed your ride with Air Marino," he chuckled.

The guy really thought he was hilarious. He would be the only one.

Katie glared him.

"Try anything and I'll kill your boyfriend," he cautioned, moving to her side and removing the handcuffs. He pulled her to a standing position.

Another man entered the cabin—the captain, Katie surmised—blond, blue-eyed and wearing a dark uniform shirt and pants.

"Take her out of here while I deal with him," The Professor instructed.

The captain walked toward her and took her arm.

"No, I won't leave without Daniel." Katie planted her feet.

"Don't worry, your boyfriend's coming too."

Katie gave Daniel one last pleading glance and reluctantly followed the captain. She turned to look over her shoulder but neither man moved.

"He'll be out in a minute," the captain said. He had a thick accent. German maybe?

She wanted to say something, but the words got stuck in her throat. Anxiousness flowed through her system, gushing adrenaline like a raging river.

A wave of thick humidity met her as she ducked through the doorway and descended the plane's steps. Katie took in the sight of the small airport empty of other planes. Only the large white hangars witnessed the scene.

A driver in black pants and jacket, complete with black cap, opened the back door of a waiting limousine.

The captain tugged her toward the car. "Get in and don't make trouble."

Katie obeyed and slid into the backseat. The new-car smell overpowered the darkness inside. She faced the window, watching the door of the plane.

Where was Daniel?

The captain slid next to her. He flipped a switch, sending a cold blast of air through the vents.

Katie shivered. "Could I get my backpack?"

"Eventually."

She turned away from the man and ran her fingers through her hair. The locket pressed against her leg and Katie instinctively knew not to draw attention to it. "What's taking them so long?"

"They'll be coming." He pulled out a gun, inspecting the magazine.

"What's that for?"

"Insurance."

NINE

Daniel sized up the man Katie had appropriately nicknamed The Professor. His neat appearance was not the attire of someone intending to do battle. He acted as though they had all the time in the world, while Daniel considered each passing second he was apart from Katie.

He yanked on the handcuffs, frustration building at the man's leisurely attitude. Too many minutes had passed since Katie had been taken from the plane. Where was she? Desperation filled his chest. He had to get to her.

"What're you waiting for? Remove these handcuffs now!"

An amused sneer crossed The Professor's face. He stood, shoulders back, head held high, yet his attempt at demonstrating confidence failed. Daniel didn't miss the radius of space he kept, or the way his gun-wielding hand shook ever so slightly. One swift attack, and he'd have the criminal unconscious and secure his newer model Sig Sauer.

"Relax. You'll be reunited in a few minutes."

A morsel of reprieve at his promise of getting to Katie lessened Daniel's panic.

As if sensing Daniel's scrutiny, the man said, "Mr. Knight, you're only alive as a courtesy. I could easily kill you and explain it as an accident."

"So, what's holding you back?"

"To be honest, I like you. You're not afraid to battle against the strongest men in the world. That takes guts. Or stupidity."

"I'm glad I impress you."

"Impress? No. Let's not get carried away. However, you do interest me. You'll find the Marino house to be…challenging. Be sure you pick the winning side."

"And what side would that be?"

"You'll figure it out. One way or the other." His smug tone fueled Daniel's agitation.

"Is that some sort of threat?"

"Take it however you wish. I'm only offering a friendly word of advice." He cautiously approached Daniel. "Remember, your girlfriend is waiting outside. Do anything stupid, and she'll be dead before you make it down the stairs. Understand?"

"I'll be as gentle as a kitten."

"Yes, you will." The man unhooked the left handcuff and jerked Daniel's arm, wrenching it backward. Pain jolted through his shoulder.

Daniel gritted his teeth.

"We won't have any trouble, will we?"

He shook with adrenaline but if the man twisted one inch higher, he'd pull Daniel's shoulder out of the socket. "No."

"Good. I'm going to release the other handcuff. If you make any sudden moves, I will shoot you."

Every part of Daniel fought the urge to jump

up and beat the man senseless. Without knowing Katie's status, he couldn't afford to take the risk.

"Get up."

Daniel pushed back from the table and got up. Once again, only Katie's safety stood in the way of him clobbering the idiot.

"Now, secure the open ends of the handcuffs around your wrists."

Daniel did as he was ordered.

The Professor used the Sig as a pointer, waving it toward the plane's open door. Daniel led the way off the aircraft, and halted at the encountered wall of humidity. He continued toward the sleek limousine while gauging his surroundings.

No surprise, the tarmac was private and empty. His gaze flew to the driver, who leaned against the rear passenger panel of the car.

Katie better be inside and unharmed. Daniel maintained a hurried clip, and The Professor struggled to keep up. That was satisfying.

The man moved around to the driver's door, and The Professor strode to talk with him. With one last glance, Daniel ducked into the cooled car's interior.

"It's been a pleasure." The Professor closed the door.

The captain and Katie sat across from Daniel; both had their backs to the driver, who was separated by a smoke glass window. The gun pressed against her head kept Daniel cemented to the seat.

Her green eyes were wide, and her lip trembled. Between the rage at seeing her in distress and his need to hold her again, Daniel shook with restraint. "Is that really necessary?"

"For her? No. For you? Yes." The man pushed the muzzle harder against her temple, and she winced.

"What would I do? You have the gun and I'm handcuffed," Daniel countered.

The captain seemed to consider that. He started to lower the weapon, then must've thought better of it. "Just in case."

"Daniel," Katie's voice shook, and she'd dug her fingernails into the seat.

"She's not the one you need to worry about." Daniel leaned forward. "Put the gun against my head."

"Sit back, or we'll finish this transaction with one less participant," the captain threatened.

"It'll all be over soon, right?" Katie's eyes pleaded with Daniel for reassurance.

The car lurched forward, causing him to teeter slightly off-balance. *That's exactly what I'm afraid of.*

The beast of a bodyguard stood in front of the open French doors. A massive gray slate patio stretched toward the ocean beyond. Floor-to-ceiling windows provided a translucent barrier to the outside world. The guard's position and the

MP5 he held prevented any attempted escape. To make matters worse, Daniel and Katie sat with their backs to the entrance of an extravagant living room, leaving them vulnerable from every direction.

Daniel had used the extended wait time to evaluate the aviator-sunglass-wearing-human obstacle. Easily two hundred pounds and six foot four. Bald with a handlebar mustache, dressed in cargo pants and military boots. Equal in physical stature, but his weapon gave the Neanderthal a serious advantage.

Comparatively, Daniel sat unarmed next to Katie. Both bound at the wrists, anxiously waiting for their fate on an expensive leather couch that cost more than his annual salary.

Hand to hand, Daniel could hold his own. Alone, he'd make a run at the guy. He wouldn't risk Katie's life trying. If he was dead, he was no use to her at all.

"How long are we going to sit here?" Daniel jerked his chin toward the motionless guard.

The man ignored the question, remaining stoic in his military attention posture.

"Why are they making us wait?" Katie whispered.

Ocean waves slammed against the shore, and the salty sea air drifted in. The sun had begun its evening descent, and hung low in the sky, filling the atmosphere with varying shades of pink, purple and orange. The view was fabulous; too bad he couldn't enjoy it for fear of their lives.

Daniel attempted to engage the bodyguard again. "What time is it?"

The man didn't move an inch.

"Thanks," Daniel snorted.

Katie shifted closer to him.

He inhaled the scent of her shampoo. *Focus on a plan of escape.*

Daniel leaned forward scanning the beach. Hard to do from this position. From what he could see, they were on Marino's private property. There were no people running around. No boats either. Which meant no help.

He'd spent the last hour flipping through his mental file cabinet, trying to remember Marino's multiple known home locations. Thanks to the kidnapper in the plane, he knew they were in Florida. Possibly on the western coastline.

The effects of the tranquilizer finally dissipated from his brain, unfortunately, no brilliant plan had sprouted.

"It's going to be okay." Katie paused. "Isn't it?"

Daniel should be the one to reassure her. He wasn't dumb enough to believe everything would be okay, and he wouldn't insult her intelligence by lying to her. Not like everyone else in her life.

The whooshing of the door behind them and three sets of footsteps on the black marble floor got Daniel's attention. He twisted to get a better visual. Katie scooted closer, her leg pressed against his.

Anthony Marino sauntered around the couch dressed in an expensive custom-fit gray suit. He was flanked by two armed ugly bodyguards.

Older looking in person than the pictures Daniel had seen, Marino's more than two decades in prison had clearly been hard ones. He moved toward a chair opposite where Daniel and Katie sat, his gaze transfixed on her.

No one spoke. Normally, that wouldn't faze Daniel, but sitting here waiting for Marino to bless them with his presence was irritating. He knew their intimidation tactics, and the silence was a feeble attempt.

Daniel wrenched his wrists, trying for the hundredth time to loosen the handcuffs, but they were securely locked.

Marino's slow gait appeared painful as he lowered himself onto the contemporary steel armchair. "It is really you, my Isabella," he crooned, leaning forward. "I apologize for the harsh manner in which you were transported here. Time is of the essence and I knew you would not come voluntarily."

"Having me attacked, kidnapped and handcuffed was hardly the way to introduce yourself into my life. And my name is Katie Tribani." Katie lifted her head higher and sat straighter.

Daniel gave her an approving nod. The last

thing she needed to do was be a cowering wimp in front of Marino.

Marino shook his head. "I would love the gift of time, but as you can see, I'm an old man and growing weaker by the day. I had to expedite your travel. It is my great desire to destroy the lies you have been raised to believe. However, if you prefer I call you Katie, I will honor your wishes."

"Not that this hasn't been fun, sitting bound for hours on end, but maybe you could remove the handcuffs?" Daniel inserted.

As if annoyed by his presence, Marino faced him. "I cannot trust you, US Marshal Daniel Knight."

"That's not very nice. You don't even know me."

"I appreciate you protecting my daughter, but like her, you have been misinformed. Until I believe you are trustworthy, I must insist upon your restraints." Marino gestured toward Katie. "Remove my daughter's handcuffs."

The smaller of the two bodyguards, a man resembled a meaty leprechaun in his bright green shirt and jeans, scurried to Katie's side, unlocking the shackles.

Katie rubbed her wrists. "Remove Daniel's handcuffs too. He won't hurt anyone."

"Yeah, I promise not to hurt anyone." Daniel made no attempt to hide his sarcasm.

Marino's lips flattened to a straight line. "No, he won't."

We'll see about that.

When Marino reached for Katie, she scooted backward and tucked her hands between her knees.

"Please, I only wish to see if you're okay," Marino cooed.

Daniel gritted his teeth as Katie complied.

Marino gently rubbed at her bruises from the cuffs then shot a venomous glare at the leprechaun bodyguard, who ducked his head and scurried back.

"Isabella." Marino kissed Katie's wrists.

She flinched, and a protective volt blasted through Daniel. "Don't you touch her."

Marino ignored him.

Daniel wanted Katie to yank her wrist free, but instead she gently pulled away.

"She doesn't know you," Daniel growled.

Marino inclined his head toward Daniel. His expression softened. "Yes, an unfortunate truth. We will change that."

"I only learned of you after Mama's death," Katie said.

"I heard of Evangelina's demise. God's punishment for her betrayal and lies," Marino hissed. As if someone slapped him, he paused; the anger quickly morphed into a mask of compassion. "Regardless of our differences, I was sorry to hear of her prolonged suffering. Let us not speak of her. Isabella, you are home now. That's all that matters."

Katie shot Daniel a glance. Confusion? Fear? She faced Marino again. "If I'm *home*, as you've said, release Daniel." She rested her hand on his arm. "He's done nothing but protect me."

Marino's eyes narrowed, but he didn't argue. "Very well, but understand, any move I deem a threat will result in shackles or worse. Am I clear, Mr. Knight?"

Daniel worked his jaw and gave a quick, one motion nod. He fought the impulse to attack the leprechaun bodyguard as he removed the handcuffs.

"Leave us," Marino barked at the two bodyguards. Both darted out of the room.

Katie gave a slight nod to the aviator-wearing guard by the glass doors.

Marino turned to follow her gaze. "That is Lorenzo. He's always with me."

"Oh," Katie said, the apprehension thick.

Good, she hadn't failed to see the issue. Marino didn't trust them. And she shouldn't trust him.

Katie kept close to Daniel's side. "So, what do you want with me?"

Marino's face was gleeful. "You're my precious daughter. I want to give you the life you deserve and remove all the lies that Jezebel of a mother poisoned you with. We've lost much time—we will make up for it now that you're here." Marino unbuttoned his suit jacket and leaned back in the chair, crossing his legs. "Perhaps it's better if we speak alone."

Why was Marino trying to get rid of him? "No way," Daniel asserted, sitting up straighter.

"She's in no danger, I assure you. Lorenzo." Marino waved the guard over. "Please take Mr. Knight to his room."

"I don't want Daniel to go," Katie argued.

"I'm afraid what I need to say isn't for him to hear. It is private." Marino turned to Lorenzo. "He will join us for dinner after I've had time to talk with Isabella."

Lorenzo moved toward Daniel, reaching for his arm.

Daniel stiffened, his glare hard. "I'm not going anywhere so either shoot me or start talking."

TEN

Katie put her hand on Daniel's leg, willing him to stay. She needed him there; his presence was not only comforting, it was essential. His muscles tensed beneath her fingers. "With all due respect," she said, gesturing around the massive room, "this is a little intimidating. Not to mention the body-guards and guns."

Anthony exhaled loudly. "Very well."

"Thank you." Would he acquiesce to a certain degree for his daughter? Might be good information for later.

Lorenzo stepped to the windows without turning his back on them.

Anthony's determination to get her alone left Katie unsettled, feeding her already increasing fear of the man. Her gaze traveled over him. He was well-dressed, clean-shaven and wore his silver-and-black hair in a short, neat style. His eyes, the same color as hers, acted like her own DNA test, confirming their familial connection. Naive perhaps, but the elder Marino's welcoming exuberance stabbed at her defenses. Yet, she didn't want to know him. Did she? Except this man was her father.

Anthony grasped her hand. "It's important that I speak with you—"

He paused, dropping her hand. His posture

grew rigid as he looked past her. Katie twisted around. A younger, taller and darker image of her father entered. Giovanni? Classy and suave in his dark dress pants and light gray sweater, he beamed a perfect Hollywood smile at her.

"So, the prodigal returns. It's great to have you home, baby sister." He moved toward Katie, pulling her upward into a hug.

Daniel inserted himself between them. Lorenzo moved forward, gun poised.

"It's okay." Katie gave Daniel a shaky smile.

He returned a wary glance before sitting down.

Lorenzo returned to his post at the door.

Katie obliged the awkward hug. "You must be Giovanni."

"I must." Giovanni's dark eyes surveyed her. He released his hold and slid onto the chair next to Anthony. "Who's he?" His politeness turned ice-cold as he regarded Daniel.

"US Marshal Daniel Knight." Daniel's voice was low and menacing.

"I thought the old guy was the marshal." Giovanni smirked at Anthony.

The man's rude callousness struck Katie.

Daniel narrowed his eyes. "Mason Garrett is *dead* thanks to your men. He was tortured for information before—" He gave Katie an apologetic grimace then looked down.

Katie gasped. "What?"

Daniel slowly lifted his head, and met her

eyes. "I'm sorry, Katie, I shouldn't have said it that way."

"Is it true? Did they torture..." Katie covered her mouth, unable to speak the rest of the sentence.

Daniel didn't answer, confirming her worst assumptions. Horror at the mere thought of Uncle Nick being hurt caused bile to rise in her throat. She swallowed hard. Maybe, he'd gotten away. Somehow. Tears welled in her eyes. "We should've gone back and helped him." She glared at the Marino men. "How could you do something so horrid?"

"I know nothing of this. My men were sent with the sheer purpose of retrieving my daughter," the older Marino defended. "These wretched allegations are more lies by your government to paint me an evil man."

Katie's gaze ping-ponged between them. Anthony's confused expression spoke his surprise while Giovanni's nonchalant manner infuriated her.

Giovanni interrupted the silence with his coldhearted comment. "I'm afraid the death of the marshal was an unfortunate accident by my men. I assure you, he was not tortured."

"You're a liar," Daniel spat.

Katie met Giovanni's eyes. He gave her a thin smile and faced Daniel. "Did you see it happen, Mr. Knight? Or were you informed by your people?"

"They have no reason to lie," Daniel said, but the conviction wasn't as strong as she'd hoped. "Murder isn't accidental."

Anthony pinned Giovanni with his inquisitive gaze. "Why would you send more men?"

"I hoped to bring my baby sister home as a surprise to you, Father. But you beat me to the task. I guess we were both anxious." Giovanni snickered.

Anthony's lips tightened. He shifted. Was he upset?

"My employees were reprimanded for their haste. Had they waited, we might have saved the trek from Starling to Manitou. You have my apologies." Giovanni offered his hand, which Daniel refused.

"I'd prefer justice," Daniel growled.

"Justice comes in many forms, Mr. Knight," Anthony answered. His green eyes darkened.

"Perhaps your men were misinformed, Daniel?" Katie needed that to be true. Prayed it so.

"No, Katie. These murderous monsters killed Mason Garrett." Daniel's gaze locked with hers.

"Have either of you seen pictures? Video? Real proof?" Giovanni quizzed.

Daniel slowly turned to face Giovanni but didn't answer.

Katie's head spun. She closed her eyes trying to eliminate the thoughts of Uncle Nick—Mason—and the dreadful images that fought for her attention. The need for real answers kept her sitting. She had to remain strong. She inhaled deeply and surveyed the room. The men postured for control. That was the least of her worries. "Could we get back to why I'm here?"

"Isabella—"

"Katie," she corrected.

Anthony folded his hands in his lap and sighed. "Yes, I suppose that is the only name you have known, my darling. Your mother's deviousness knew no bounds. Even to remove your Christian name."

Katie chose her words with care. "My mother was a wonderful woman. I will thank you not to speak of her in any way other than pure respect, Mr. Marino."

Anthony's lips flattened. "Please, call me Anthony until you feel comfortable calling me Father."

"Anthony, as I said, I only learned of you after my mother's death. I haven't even had a chance to grieve her loss. One day I'm sitting in my living room crying, the next I'm handed..."

Daniel shifted against her, his movement invisible except to her. She caught the warning and her gut agreed. The increasing weight of the locket solidified its existence.

Anthony quirked an eyebrow and leaned forward. "You were saying?"

"One minute I'm reading my mother's obituary in the morning paper." She gave herself a mental high-five for a quick recovery. "The next, I'm being rushed out and men are shooting at me."

"What?" Anthony stood, his hands fisted. "Who shot at you?"

"Again, Father, it was a misunderstanding," Giovanni cajoled, resting a hand on his father's back.

"That's no excuse! She could have been killed!" Anthony's face reddened.

"Yes." Giovanni waved his hand as if he were shooing a pesky fly. "That would have been terrible."

Anthony slumped back. Not the mannerisms of a heartless crime lord, more like an elderly parent.

"Yes, Giovanni. Do explain how your men *accidentally* shot at us in Nebraska at the safe house, the airport *and* in Colorado on the Manitou Incline," Daniel disputed.

Katie glanced between her father and brother. Giovanni fisted his hands over the arms of the chair. His eyes sparked as he reclined. "Again, they were misinformed. You have my *apology* for the miscommunication."

His poised demeanor didn't disguise the venom darting from Giovanni's narrowed eyes. He collected himself, but his arrogance said he wasn't used to being questioned.

"How does one misinform another about killing someone versus kidnapping? Autocorrect on a text message?" Katie snapped.

Giovanni's lips twitched into a tight smile, and for a second, his eyes flashed. Then, as if a drain plug had been pulled, all the displayed tension flowed into the distinguished pose he wore like a coat.

"Would someone start telling me truth?" Katie demanded.

Anthony sighed. "Evangelina stole you from our home and in a heartless gesture, left behind poor Giovanni."

Katie flicked a glance at Giovanni, who looked anything but poor. His jaw flexed at the mention of her mother.

Anthony's voice increased in volume. "She lied to the Feds, and I was falsely incarcerated."

"What did she tell them that put you in prison?" Katie inquired.

A look passed between Giovanni and Anthony. "It doesn't matter. I have forgiven her. She was a troubled woman."

"Why didn't you send someone to come for me?" The blurted words escaped before she could censor them.

"I tried, child. But Mason Garrett," he spat the last word, "stole my wife and daughter from me. I believe they were romantically involved."

"They most certainly were not! Mama never even dated anyone," Katie defended. She might be angry at Mama's choices in hiding the truth from her, but she wasn't going to allow these two strangers to slander the only parent she'd ever known.

Anthony's shoulders lowered, deflating his angry steam. He paused. A look of bewilderment crossed his face. "Mason Garrett didn't assume a fatherly role in your life?"

Katie gaped. "Are you kidding? I knew him as Uncle Nick until yesterday. They never had a romantic relationship. In fact, until yesterday I believed they'd grown up together in a foster home. They always behaved as brother and sister. He lived in his own house in town."

"Interesting." Anthony's relief was palpable. "At any rate, it wasn't until the picture of her obituary came up that I discovered your location. *Nebraska*, of all places."

"I'd say that makes you the *poor thing*." Giovanni's condescending chuckle infuriated Katie.

"Starling was a wonderful place to grow up," she snapped.

Anthony stood. "You're tired. There will be time to talk and I'm sure you need to freshen up before dinner. I apologize for my men's lack of gallantry and Giovanni's lack of communication."

Giovanni glowered at his father. The look faded and he was again the picture of demeanor and class.

"Ah, timely as always." Anthony held out his hand.

Confused, Katie turned. A stout woman with gray hair pinned in a low bun and dressed in a traditional housekeeper's uniform entered. She trotted straight to Anthony's side.

Anthony put his arm around her shoulders. "This is Priscilla. She takes great care of us. My most trusted and faithful assistant. And Giovanni's childhood nanny."

"More like a pest," Giovanni mumbled.

Katie jerked her head toward him.

He covered his mouth, muting his fake cough.

The woman either hadn't heard his comment or ignored it, because she beamed at the older Marino's praise. Wrinkles around her eyes implied she laughed a lot. She had beautiful sun-kissed skin and wore sensible black shoes that complimented the uniform. Everything about her gave off a gentle maternal vibe.

"She will show you both to your rooms. Dinner will be served in an hour. Will that give you enough time?" Anthony asked.

Time for what? It wasn't as if she had luggage to choose an outfit from. Anthony's quick dismissal had Katie questioning what he was hiding, and from whom. Giovanni? "Yes. That would be fine."

"Your room has been supplied with clothes and

toiletries. If you need anything, Priscilla will help you," Anthony stated.

"It's really you," Priscilla exclaimed, reaching for Katie and pulling her into a hug. "Ah, Bella. You're more beautiful than I remember."

Katie liked her immediately and relaxed in the embrace. Priscilla could be a complete fake, but everything within her wanted to believe in the woman's genuineness.

"And you are?" Priscilla released Katie and turned to address Daniel.

"Daniel Knight, ma'am." He shook her hand.

Daniel's kindness toward Priscilla endeared him even more to Katie.

"Welcome, Daniel. Come, come. We'll get you all set." Priscilla grabbed Katie's hand and led her out of the living room. Daniel trailed close behind. "It's so good to have you home."

"Remember your place, Priscilla. This isn't *your* home to welcome them into," Giovanni bit. "You're nothing but the maid."

The trio stopped and turned.

"Giovanni!" Anthony bellowed.

Though the rebuke wasn't aimed at her, Katie's ears warmed. She could slap Giovanni. The smug expression he wore like a trophy proved he'd meant to hurt the older woman, increasing Katie's outrage.

Priscilla's shoulders drooped. "Yes, you're so

right, Mr. Giovanni. My apologies for overstepping. I'll not make the mistake again."

Katie didn't miss the sorrow in the elder woman's expression. More than receiving rebuke, it was the look of deep regret. What had gone on in this house?

Daniel glowered at Giovanni. Katie must have sensed his irritation because she wrapped her arm in his, and pulled him along behind Priscilla.

The sweet housekeeper chattered while he surveyed the enormous house, built and paid for with crimes and blood money. They walked through a long hallway and an immense foyer. The front door's intricate smoked glass design allowed the light to penetrate while casting a kaleidoscope across the white marble floor.

Daniel and Katie followed Priscilla up the staircase, winding from one side of the foyer to the other. Giovanni watched below. Every instinct in Daniel's body blared on high alert.

Priscilla chattered on about Florida, making small talk with Katie. Daniel appreciated the distraction. He needed to come up with an escape plan. His gaze flitted to the housekeeper and an idea sprouted to life. What was better than someone with insider knowledge?

When they'd reached the top of the staircase, Priscilla led them down a never-ending hallway with closed doors on both sides. They were out of Giovanni's or Lorenzo's hearing range.

"I'm sorry about how Giovanni treated you back there," he interrupted.

The older woman paused and pivoted. "Oh, honey, he didn't treat me wrong. Mr. Giovanni is a kind and wonderful man. It was my fault for forgetting my place. I tend to do that. Old age setting in."

"Does he do that often?" Daniel probed in a softer tone, drawing closer to Priscilla.

She tilted her head. "Do what, hon?"

"Belittle you," Katie inserted.

"Oh, he doesn't mean anything by it." Priscilla worked her apron over her fingers. "Don't fret yourself over such things. Come on, there's so much left to show you."

"This is quite the home," Daniel said.

"Uh-huh," Katie responded with a wide-eyed expression.

"Yes, indeed," Priscilla cooed.

Daniel touched her arm. "If it wouldn't get you into any trouble, could I have my gun back?"

"Oh, yes, and my backpack?" Katie asked.

Priscilla stopped at a door in the center of the hallway. "Gun? Oh, hon, you don't need that here. You're safe." Lowering her voice, she said, "I'll see about the bag."

Daniel smiled his appreciation. Though he wasn't pleased with the arrangement, it was progress and it showed Priscilla was amenable to their requests.

Priscilla pushed open an oversize white door revealing a bedroom the size of his apartment.

He took in the expensive decorations and contemporary-styled furniture that included a king-size bed with a dark brown leather pillow headboard and cream duvet.

He turned to see Katie's reaction.

Her mouth gaped as she ran her hand along the foot of the bed.

Nightstands made of a light wood on either side of the bed held decorative brushed nickel lamps. Floor-to-ceiling windows were veiled behind sheer curtains. Cream drapes pulled back on either side by white cord tiebacks matched the duvet.

He'd expected basement prison cell accommodations, so everything about the place surprised Daniel. He reminded himself that Marino's nefarious dealings paid for his life of comfort.

Priscilla moved to a large armoire positioned at the opposite wall and opened the doors. Inside a flat-screen TV sat on a pedestal. She pulled out several of the drawers. "Mr. Marino provided you with essentials." She lifted a few shirts and sweatpants to illustrate her comment. "I do hope they fit."

Daniel squeezed out a polite, "Thank you." He'd reserve his rude comments for the Marinos.

"This is incredible," Katie exhaled.

Priscilla pointed to a door, explaining it was the bathroom. "Let's go see your bedroom, Bella."

"As lovely as all of this is, Katie and I won't be staying through the evening." Daniel glanced out the window.

"Mr. Knight, don't be silly. You just arrived. Please take the necessary time to clean up before dinner. Make yourself comfortable and Lorenzo will come for you when it's time."

Daniel turned to see Priscilla tug Katie out of the room.

"Wait!" He ran toward the women, missing them by inches as the door closed, followed by a subsequent click. He gripped the handle and tugged. Convenient. The lock was on the outside. Daniel pounded on the door. "Katie!"

He slumped against the door. His emotions danced between humor at being outsmarted by the sweet housekeeper, and annoyance for allowing it. More than that, Katie's absence made him want to blast through the walls to reach to her.

Daniel reminded himself Marino didn't bring him here to kill him. At least, he hoped not. His emerging personal feelings about Katie had to be squelched because those distractions weren't what either of them needed to escape this place.

Might as well make the most of the time. He moved through the room, checking for bugs, cameras or anything else intrusive.

Neither of the nightstand drawers held anything

except the remote control for the television set. He walked over and pulled back the sheer drapes, revealing the single-paned window. Of course, it wouldn't open.

He looked out at the ocean crashing onto the shore beneath. Anthony's bodyguards he'd met earlier in the living room stood on the slate patio. They waved with the distinction of two participants riding a float in the Macy's Thanksgiving Day Parade, reminding him there was no escaping this place.

ELEVEN

Daniel's bedroom door lock clicked, and Giovanni entered. "Sorry about keeping you secured. It's precautionary."

"Really, for what?" Daniel closed the distance between them. Giovanni was unarmed but doubtful the man was alone.

Giovanni pushed the door closed. "Because you'd love to drag my little sister from us again. We needed to be sure you couldn't do that. Priscilla is an old woman who you'd easily overpower. I advised her to lock the door."

"I'm a guest with no privileges like a phone or windows that open? Sounds more like a prisoner." Daniel stood feet shoulder-width apart, arms crossed.

"Guess it's what you make of it. You know, Isabella—"

"Katie."

"*My sister's* home. Your services are no longer needed."

"I guess we'll see about that. How long do you plan to keep us against our will?"

"You are free to go, Mr. Knight. Without Isabella. In all honesty, it would be better if you left."

"I won't leave her."

"Then we're not keeping you against your will, are we? You're choosing to stay here. As for your weapons, I might consider returning them. After we've established you're not a threat. You can't blame me for being cautious." Giovanni sighed. "You're here as our guest, but if you cause any problems, or try to take my little sister away, I'll be forced to take care of you…permanently."

"Is that a threat?"

Giovanni's sardonic laugh accentuated his words. "Threats are for schoolyard fights." He crossed the room, stopping inches from Daniel's face. "Be good, Marshal Man. Or you'll no longer be welcome here."

Daniel stepped closer. "My only allegiance is to Katie."

"Yes, you do appear… What's the word? Loyal. Like a dog." Giovanni turned away from Daniel. "My men were instructed to kill you, but they were clearly incapable. No worry about that. I won't tolerate incompetence. They've been punished for their inability to complete the simple mission."

"Your father didn't appear to appreciate your interference."

"My father is senile and unable to think clearly. He insisted on bringing you here, but I haven't figured out why."

"Make it easy on me. Give me back my gun, and I'll call a cab."

Giovanni turned to face Daniel, a smirk on his *GQ* face. "If I bought that line, we'd both be idiots." He turned and stared out the window. "I know a lot about you, Daniel Knight."

"I guess that makes us even. I know plenty about you too."

"I'll always be a step ahead. Just like I knew where to find you every time you made some feeble attempt to get away."

Daniel took the bait. "That was convenient. Tell me, who's the mole in my office?"

Giovanni chuckled. "Let's say I'm very persuasive when I need to be."

"Were they bought? Threatened?" Daniel pressed.

"A gentleman never kisses and tells," Giovanni said. "Suffice it to say, whatever illusions you have of protecting Isabella are just that, illusions. Go away and let us rebuild our family. Your government did a lifetime of damage. Even you can't deny that."

"You must have a hearing problem, so let me say it again. I'm not going anywhere. Katie's isn't naive enough to buy into this innocent businessman routine."

"Maybe not, but what concern is that to you?" Giovanni brushed past Daniel and leaned against the wall. He crossed his ankles and put his hands into his pockets. A terrific model pose for his fake world. "I am a businessman, as you've so conveniently stated, and I understand the need for a good deal. Leave us, and I'll make it worth your while. You and I are more alike than you think. I know what it's like to want to reunite family. To wonder every day if she's safe."

Giovanni grinned, and Daniel shifted uncomfortably. What was the maniac saying?

"Mr. Knight, I can help you find what you've been looking for all these years."

Daniel smirked allowing the full depth of his sarcasm to ooze through his words. "Oh, yeah, and what could you possibly think I need to find?"

"Brittany."

He struggled not to show the emotions threatening to surface. Daniel wouldn't give Giovanni the satisfaction. He swallowed the lump in his throat. "You don't have a clue where my sister is."

"Don't I?"

"Unlike your family, we don't kidnap and drag members of my family back home. Brittany is capable of returning when she wants to." Daniel worked to increase the confidence in his tone, but the temptation hung in the air.

"You're not thinking clearly. I'm sure the tranquilizers are still fogging your brain. Take some time to consider my offer. Isabella would never need to know why you left. I'll cover for you. You can return to your meager life as a marshal, and bring peace to your own family by rescuing your sister."

Giovanni's arrogance was annoying.

"You don't know anything about my family,"

Daniel said. “Interesting that you used the word rescue. Do you also have my sister hostage?”

Giovanni ignored the question. “She’s had her share of problems. A confused young woman. She asked about you.”

Daniel lunged, grabbing Giovanni by the shoulders and slamming him against the wall. “If you lay a hand on my sister—”

“Now, now, Mr. Knight. Threats don’t work with me. Remember, I have too much to bargain with.”

Daniel shoved him away. “Tell me where she is.”

“I’d love to. But as I said, I need something in return.” Giovanni spun on his heel and walked toward the door. “Brittany’s drug habit is quite sad. How can anyone with a brain buy into the lie that a substance means more than her own flesh and blood.”

Daniel glared at Giovanni’s smooth-as-a-baby’s-bottom face. “You’re beyond a hypocrite. It’s scum like you that provide drugs on the streets, trapping people like Brittany. Don’t you dare pretend to sympathize when you’re the monster that lured her into misery.”

“You give me too much credit. I wouldn’t dream of providing illegal drugs on the streets of America.” Giovanni sneered. “I can understand your irrational thoughts, however. Your sister needs your help. Ponder my proposal.” He opened the door, exposing Lorenzo on the other side, cradling the MP5. "See you at dinner."

The men walked away from the room, leaving the door open.

A test? Daniel waited a few seconds before peering down the hallway where Lorenzo stood with a stupid grin plastered on his ugly mug.

Giovanni's deception was evident every time he opened his mouth, and that loving brother act didn't sit well. The man was a beacon of arrogance and wickedness. Being in the Marino home was like standing in the lion's den waiting to be attacked.

Daniel's stomach tightened at the impossible situation with no winning choices.

Giovanni was providing a way for him to get Brittany home. Years of searching would be over. Wondering. Worrying.

He couldn't fathom abandoning Katie to the mercy of two psychopaths. If he left, who knew what the Marinos would do. Daniel closed his eyes. The truth was he couldn't imagine never again seeing Katie Tribani. The reality was a high-speed transaction from his head to his heart. The little brunette had invaded his defenses more than he cared to admit, and there was no denying he'd do anything for her.

Yet, if he stayed, what would happen to Brittany?

Katie sat on the bed, fingering the dusty rose evening gown. She looked down at her jeans again, debating whether to change into the dress that Priscilla had insisted—no, begged—her to wear. The maid seemed confused when Katie refused and offered her the choice of a different gown instead.

The bedroom closet was filled with beautiful designer outfits and she'd almost given in to Priscilla's request, until she noticed all of the clothes were in her size.

She shivered at the realization that her father had somehow managed to find out such personal information long before she'd arrived. Did the man have any inkling how invasive and creepy that was?

Daniel's absence convinced Katie she'd do just about anything to get back to his side. It wasn't just having him there to protect her. Though he made her feel safe in ways she couldn't describe. It was as if Daniel grounded her. Gave her a center of gravity. Had it not been for Priscilla's assurances that he was safe and would join her in minutes, Katie would be beating a hole through the wall to get to him.

She paced between the closet and her bed, clutching the locket in her hand. She needed a hiding place. The safe? No. Why would Anthony offer her a place to secure things, knowing full well she hadn't brought anything with her? No doubt they'd gone through the backpack—which still hadn't been returned to her. It wasn't as if it had anything of value, but she detested that they'd taken it away.

Maybe the safest place for the locket was in her possession. She tucked the necklace back into her pocket and pulled the oversize hoodie down around her hips.

The latch clicked, jolting Katie. She rushed to the door, anxious to be released from the confines of the bedroom.

Lorenzo's massive presence filled the doorway. Head shaking with disapproval in his expression, he shifted to the side. Relief coursed through her at the sight of Daniel in the hallway. He was still dressed in his cargo pants and a black T-shirt. She wasn't the only one who'd refused the clothing offers.

Katie squeezed past the bodyguard and moved to Daniel's side, inhaling his scent like oxygen filling her lungs. "Am I ever glad to see you. It's a good thing I'm not claustrophobic because being locked in that room wasn't fun."

"Tell me about it." His eyes met hers, and she didn't look away.

Lorenzo poked at them with his gun, motioning toward the stairs. "Let's go."

"Really?" Katie shot him a glare.

"Guess it's time for dinner." Daniel placed his hand against the small of her back, and stayed close to her side, leading her down the staircase.

Lorenzo's silent, intimidating presence lingered behind them.

Priscilla stood at the doorway and waved them over. She frowned as they drew closer. "Bella, did the dress not fit you?"

"I'm sure it would have, but I'm more comfortable in my own clothes," Katie said.

The maid's eyebrows furrowed and she pursed her lips together. "I hope you'll reconsider."

Daniel led Katie through the doorway, and into the dining room. She took in the elegant space, holding tightly to his arm.

The far wall was made entirely of windows overlooking the ocean. White-and-black chairs surrounded the rectangular smoked glass table positioned in the center of the room. A stone fireplace covered one wall and two spherical glass chandeliers hung from the ceiling, casting soft light. Anthony sat at the head of the table with Giovanni to his right. Both were dressed in suits and deep in conversation that ceased as she and Daniel entered the room.

Anthony's obvious disapproval was written in the frown on his face. "Did Priscilla not instruct you to dress for dinner?"

Katie turned but Priscilla wasn't with them. "She did."

"Then what's the problem?" Giovanni inserted.

Daniel's arm tensed beneath her fingers. She squeezed gently aiming her reply at Anthony. "Although I'm sure you meant well, I find it disconcerting that you purchased clothing in my size before I'd even arrived."

Anthony's eyes narrowed, enhancing the gray shadows on his face. "Shouldn't a father provide for his family? I hoped to surprise you with the best gifts since I've not had that opportunity throughout your life. I meant no offense and hope you'll reconsider my generosity."

Daniel snorted. "Why don't you start by giving us the freedom to leave this place?"

"I agree," Katie chimed in.

Anthony steepled his fingers on the table. "As much as I understand your desire to leave, Bella, I must insist you stay. You've been misled into believing lies. I want the chance to clear up those misunderstandings. If I let you leave, you'll never return."

"That would be a shame," Giovanni inserted. One side of his lips inched upward and he took a sip from his crystal goblet.

Katie swallowed. "Shouldn't I have the freedom to make that decision? Wouldn't you rather have me here because I want to be, not because you're forcing me?"

"Right now, I will take the former because it is what is best for you."

"You don't know anything about me." Katie's cheeks warmed, and she worked to keep her tone calm. "And you can't keep me here forever."

Lorenzo stepped forward and tapped his fingers lightly on the MP5.

Anthony sighed and gestured toward the table. "Please, sit."

"I don't think we have a choice, Daniel," Katie replied.

His scowl mimicked her thoughts. They walked to the left side of the room and sat across from Giovanni.

An awkward silence filled the room. Katie didn't appreciate the way neither man addressed Daniel. She sat and took a sip of water from the crystal goblet, grateful he remained close to her side.

A maid entered, pushing a rolling serving cart with covered platters. The thin blonde, in her early twenties, wore a uniform similar to Priscilla's. In contrast, this woman's clothing contoured her body in a snug, revealing fashion. Her hair was short and pulled back in a tight ponytail. She was attractive even with the excessive amount of makeup she wore.

She set a silver-domed plate in front of Katie, and offered a thin-lipped smile. With expert precision she removed the cover, revealing a thick steak, mashed potatoes and grilled vegetables.

Katie met Daniel's eyes and lifted an eyebrow. He gave her slight nod and mouthed the word *wait*. She lifted her glass and smiled, acknowledging the silent advice. She resisted the delicious smells wafting from the plate, while her stomach begged she dive in.

The maid delivered the remaining platters, with Giovanni's being the last.

"Thank you, Tiffany. Always a delight to be in your care." His obvious flirting made Katie uncomfortable.

Tiffany appeared thrilled by the attention and giggled as she exited. Giovanni's leering gaze focused on her the entire time.

"Please enjoy," Anthony announced.

"Before we do that," Daniel interrupted. "What's my assurance that our food isn't poisoned?"

Giovanni snickered. "If you're concerned, we can swap plates, Mr. Knight. We might be wealthy, but we wouldn't waste good food trying to kill you off."

Daniel stood, carried his plate to Giovanni and exchanged the meals.

Katie watched the interaction, noting Giovanni's smug grin. "Here, Daniel, let's exchange," she offered.

"That's not necessary," Anthony snapped.

"Why not?" Daniel asked, holding both plates.

"If you're to be in our home, you need to have some measure of trust. I assure you, the goal was not to bring you here and poison you. Please do not insult my generosity any further." Anthony's aged face took on an element of exhaustion.

Daniel didn't move for several seconds.

"Relax, Mr. Knight. Take whichever plate you prefer, but please sit down and stop hindering this lovely meal," Giovanni said.

Daniel exchanged plates with Katie and sat down.

The group dug into the meal, and the clatter of silverware against the fine china filled the room.

Between bites, Katie looked from her brother to her father. She forced herself to eat slowly and use all her best manners. When most of her dinner had been consumed, she spoke. "Mr. Marino—"

"Please, call me Anthony," he requested.

"Anthony, I'm not sure how to say this without it coming out wrong."

"Offending us doesn't seem to be an issue to you. Why worry about that now?" Giovanni asked.

Katie shot a glare at him.

"Go ahead. You can ask me anything, even if it comes out wrong." Anthony dabbed at his mouth with the crimson cloth napkin.

"As much as I appreciate the extravagance you've offered, you understand that I can't stay here." Katie looked at Daniel.

He leaned forward facing Anthony.

An unbearable second ticked by.

Anthony sighed and set down his silverware. "It's no secret I've done horrible things in my past. I'm sure Mr. Knight has provided details for you." He didn't appear angry, instead, his eyes were sad.

Katie shook her head. "He—"

"I paid for those things in prison. I'm a changed man. Evangelina was troubled and paranoid. Though she embellished to the prosecution, her delusions defined her perception. They failed to allow evidence of her institutionalization. They wanted to believe her lies." Anthony sipped his water.

Katie blinked several times. Had she heard Anthony correctly? "Mama was institutionalized?" *This man's irrational. Although... Mama did have those few bouts of depression.*

"Several times. I never dreamed she'd take you away though." Anthony lifted his silverware again.

"Funny, I've never heard of anything like that," Daniel challenged. "Since we're sharing stories, Giovanni, why don't you tell Katie about the time you tried to drown her?"

Giovanni choked on his forkful of food. When he stopped coughing, he swiped at his face with his napkin, focusing on Katie. "Is that what our mother told you?"

Katie shook her head. What was Daniel talking about?

Her sibling's reptilian eyes narrowed. "I see. More fabrications. Though I'm sure you're only regurgitating what you've been erroneously taught. Let me tell you the true version of that tale."

"You seem to think the government has a lot of time to craft tales," Daniel baited.

Giovanni leaned back and placed both of his palms on the table. "We were children, playing in the pool. You slid through your floatation device, a duck-shaped thing I think, and went under. I tried to help. As simple as that. I can't imagine how it went from a childhood accident to me trying to kill you." He stabbed at a piece of steak.

Anthony cleared his throat, aiming his words at Katie, but kept his gaze on Giovanni. "Your brother understands the need for clarification from your lifetime of deception."

Tiffany entered again, interrupting the uncomfortable dinner.

Katie rested her hands in her lap as the maid exchanged her dinner with a dessert plate. Chocolate cake topped with chocolate shavings.

"I'm happy you're home." Giovanni smiled, lifting his goblet. "Here's to the beginning of family."

"Indeed," Anthony said, holding his glass. "To family."

Daniel remained silent.

Katie halfheartedly lifted her glass and took a sip, unable to speak the word *family.*

TWELVE

The crashing waves and thick, humid air soothed Katie. A full moon hovered in the onyx sky, glowing over the ocean. The light breeze caressed her skin. All of it created the perfect background for a romantic dreamy night—except for Lorenzo's intimidating presence and that stupid gun. Both reminded Katie this dream was a nightmare.

She lounged in the Adirondack chair closest to the iron railing and fingered one of the many leafy plants bordering the slate patio. Decorative sconces hung on the outer walls of the home and light fixtures along the railing cast a soft illumination around them. "Thank you for speaking up at dinner."

Daniel faced her, glaring at Lorenzo. "There's no good way to ask if we're about to be poisoned."

"I guess they had a point. Why bring us here to kill us? They could've had Lorenzo take care of that," she whispered.

The corners of Daniel's lip lifted slightly only to be replaced by a scowl and defensive stance. Katie twisted around in her seat. Anthony exited the house, his gait slow and steady as he approached them.

Well, it was almost a pleasant evening. She sat up straighter.

Anthony dropped into the chair beside her. "Are you enjoying yourself?"

Katie gawked at his question. Did he really think this was a vacation for her? How was she supposed to answer that? She'd already offended him at dinner, a second offense wouldn't provide any benefit. "You have a beautiful home. I'm curious, what does your business do to provide such elegant surroundings?"

Anthony shook his head, ignoring her statement. "I have forgotten to be thankful for many things, Bella." He cringed. "I'm sorry. Katie. Forgive me, I'm learning to use the name you prefer."

If she didn't know better, she'd think the man was a kind, elderly gentleman. Katie tilted her head. "It's okay. Bella's starting to grow on me."

"Thank you for indulging an old man." He smiled.

"Where's Giovanni?" Daniel asked.

"He had business to attend. Such a workaholic," Anthony said. "But it is good because I have some things I must talk with you about. Mr. Knight, perhaps you'd excuse us?"

Daniel moved to Katie's side before Anthony finished the request. His chin lifted in defiance. "Nope."

"I trust Daniel with my life. You can speak freely in front of him." Katie pivoted in the seat, setting her feet down on the balcony floor. "You could send Lorenzo away though. That gun is unnerving."

Anthony sighed, turning his back to Daniel. "I cannot do that. Pretend Lorenzo is not there."

Right. That's totally possible to do.

"We've lost so much over the years. Memories that can never be replaced. Money can buy many things—too bad time isn't one of them." The wrinkles around his green eyes increased with the downturn of his lips and he looked away.

Katie waited for Anthony to continue, but he didn't speak. In the fading light, a tear weaved through the crevices of his worn face. She gripped the sides of the chair, battling the impulse to give in to the man's tenderness and vulnerability.

"I'm dying, Bella. It's why I had to kidnap you to bring you home. Forgive me for my desperate methods." Anthony shook his head.

Katie struggled to find words to respond to the report. The news didn't shock her as much as Anthony probably thought it would. The elder Marino's demeanor and coloring were evidence of his condition.

"My weak heart is giving out. The doctors have told me to set my affairs in order."

"I'm sorry to hear that." Katie shifted her glance to Daniel.

He gave a slight shake of his head.

Was Anthony lying about his heart condition? She focused on her father and softened her tone. "As much as I understand your desire for a reunion. The aggressive, death-threatening method was over-the-top."

"Giovanni—" Anthony sighed. "His impatience impedes his common sense. I don't know what I'd have done if they'd hurt you or worse." He clenched his fist.

"I'm sure if Daniel hadn't been there, I would be dead." Annoyance returned as she recalled the past twenty-four hours.

"I do appreciate that, Mr. Knight, however, I'm sure you can understand my reluctance to trust anyone involved with law enforcement." Anthony leaned back in his chair.

"No problem. The feeling's mutual with ex-cons," Daniel grunted. "I can't help but wonder why you've allowed me to be here. It's not like we're all going to live happily-ever-after under your roof."

Happily ever after with Daniel? Katie focused on the ocean waves, otherwise her imagination might take her places she couldn't afford to go.

Anthony frowned, red-faced. His words were spoken in a tight, clipped manner. "I tolerate your presence only because my daughter has requested it. Don't ever forget that."

Still didn't explain why he'd brought Daniel here in the first place.

A long pause with only the water's background noise filled the air between them.

Anthony turned to Katie, breaking the silence. "You are more lovely than I imagined. You remind me of my mother."

Curiosity overran Katie's caution. "My grandmother? Are there pictures of her?"

Priscilla walked out on the deck, moving to Anthony's side. "Such a perfect evening. I came to see if you would like anything?"

"Yes, please have Tiffany bring me a glass of ice water. And would you be so kind as to retrieve the family photo albums?" Anthony asked.

Katie nodded. "I'd love a glass of water, please."

"Mr. Knight?" Priscilla tilted her head.

"No, thank you," Daniel said.

"Very well, I'll be back in a jiffy." Priscilla disappeared into the house and returned a few minutes later with the black photo album.

"Grazie." Anthony took the album with both hands.

Tiffany sashayed out carrying a tray with drinks. "Mr. Knight, I brought a glass for you, in case you changed your mind."

Katie didn't miss how she brushed against Daniel's side, placing the beverages on the table between them.

"That'll be all," Priscilla interjected.

Tiffany glanced over her shoulder, meeting Katie's eyes. She lightly caressed Daniel's arm. "Let me know if you need anything."

The maid's flirtatious tone ignited an unexpected spark of jealousy, and Katie stiffened.

"Yeah, thanks." Daniel lifted a glass from the tray.

The insecurity disappeared as he met Katie's eyes, handing the drink to her.

"Come on, Tiffany," Priscilla called from the doorway.

The young maid turned with a raised eyebrow, flashed a cold smile to Katie and retreated to the house.

What was that about? "May I?" Katie motioned to the book.

"Yes, yes, please." A sparkle danced in Anthony's eyes.

She reached over and pulled the album onto her lap. *Marino* was embossed in gold on the black leather cover. She took care flipping the delicate pages and stopped on a black-and-white wedding picture.

Anthony leaned closer to her, placing his rough leathery finger on the picture. "Those are my grandparents, Valentina and Roberto."

"They make a stunning couple." Katie traced their faces before turning the page.

She stopped and stared at the picture of a striking young woman with eyes like Anthony's, though the black and white provided no color.

"This is my mother, Sabine. She married Valentina and Roberto's son, Francesco." Anthony smiled. "She was a strong woman. Elegant. Controlled. Never raised her voice or a hand to me. Although, I deserved it many times." He chuckled.

"I wish I'd known her."

"You did, when you were little. Your sweet face lit up when Grandmamma held you. She could send you into a fit of giggles. Such a precious memory for me. She adored you."

"She did?" Katie murmured. Why couldn't she remember her grandmother? A double loss pricked her heart. She'd known and been known but couldn't remember any of it.

"Grandmamma lived with us after my father passed. She was heartbroken when Evangelina took you away. You were only a toddler, still learning to talk and teetering on chubby little legs." Anthony's gaze hardened.

Katie contemplated his explanation. No one could truly know another's heart. Was it possible he'd changed? Giovanni admitted to sending the men with guns, right? She caught a glimpse of Daniel in her peripheral vision and shook off the sentimental nonsense. No, Anthony was a criminal, and Mama deliberately left for that reason.

Anthony interrupted her thoughts, "Do not let your heart become hard, Bella. It's not worth holding grudges. Gives you wrinkles." He emphasized his point by waggling his thick eyebrows, and smiling. But the grin didn't reach his eyes. "Look at it this way, I'll never have to ground you for being naughty."

She grinned despite her reservations.

The ocean waves crashed in the distance, rhythmic and comforting in their timekeeping.

Anthony leaned forward, his tone low. "Bella, I'm sorry to intrude into your privacy, but I must ask, did your mother give you a necklace? A special locket, perhaps?"

"Why would that matter?" Daniel inserted, reminding them of his presence.

"It's personal, Mr. Knight," Anthony answered dryly.

Katie maintained a blank expression. "A locket?"

Anthony blew out a breath and nodded. "Yes. I gave it to your mother on our wedding night. Ironically, the locket was already engraved with the letter *E* in the center. Almost as if it had been created just for Evangelina."

"It wasn't made for Mama?"

"No, it's a priceless heirloom rumored to have belonged to the queen of Italy. It has been in our family for generations."

"No way." Katie clamped her mouth shut.

"She never showed it to you?" Anthony probed.

"I can honestly say she never wore or talked about anything like that," Katie offered. *Nice recovery and not a lie.*

"I know she took it when she left. Perhaps she sold it," Anthony said.

"Let me guess, you want it back?" Daniel asked. "Is that the real reason you dragged us here?"

Anthony scowled at Daniel. "Mr. Knight, must you always speak with such disdain? And why must you poke your nose into our business? This doesn't concern you."

"Funny thing, being kidnapped and held here at gunpoint has given me a whole new perspective on what's my business."

The tension was as thick as the humidity.

Katie studied her father's aged face, framed by his thick salt-and-pepper hair, making him look distinguished.

"Are you sure you've never seen the locket?" He asked his penetrating gaze fixed on Katie.

"So what if she had?" Daniel asked.

Thank you. Katie caught a glimpse of Lorenzo in her peripheral vision. He still wore those ridiculous aviator sunglasses, hiding whatever he might be focused on. Was he listening?

Anthony ignored Daniel and returned to the album, flipping to a wedding picture. "I'd forgotten how captivating Evangelina is…was… I fell in love with her the day we met, you know." He ran his fingers over the photo. "That was the happiest day of my life. Until you were born."

Interesting he didn't say the same about Giovanni.

Anthony leaned next to Katie, and whispered, "I understand that you don't trust me. Why should you? But, my darling, if you do know about the necklace, remember it is priceless. Precious. It must be guarded…even from Giovanni. He's lived with a terrible anger and need for revenge since your mother left. I did my best to help him to move past it, but he holds a grudge. There is a secret compartment in your bedroom, beneath the closet floor—"

"Priscilla showed me," Katie interrupted. "Remember I came with nothing since my backpack was taken from me."

"I will make sure it's returned." Anthony searched her eyes.

"I'd appreciate that," Katie said.

"I'd like my gun back too," Daniel interjected.

Anthony turned, pinning Daniel with a scowl. "That will not happen." He returned his focus to Katie. "Giovanni is goal-driven with a great eye for details. He'll do whatever it takes to get what he wants, even to the degree of being ruthless. His biggest weakness is that he fails to see the human component in business relations. That's where you come in. You will be the softer side of Marino Industries."

"Let me get this straight, you brought Katie here to run the family business—which we all know is made up of human trafficking, drugs and weapons—knowing it would put her closer to danger?" Daniel assessed.

A chill slithered up Katie's back. Her mouth went dry.

"No, I brought her here because I need her help," Anthony growled.

Katie noticed he didn't dispute Daniel's accusations. *So, it was true.*

Daniel straightened, and focused over Katie's shoulder. Mockery was evident in his tone, "Hello, Giovanni. We are so glad you could join us."

"There you are. Did I miss much?" He sauntered toward the trio.

Katie turned. How long had he been there?

"No, I was just learning some of our family history and looking at old pictures." Katie's words rushed out more enthusiastically than necessary.

Giovanni dropped down into the only available chair. "Find anything valuable?"

Was it her imagination or did he emphasize *valuable*?

"No, but it was a delight to tell Bella about Grandmamma," Anthony responded.

Giovanni snickered. "Not much worth telling."

The smile faded from Anthony's face.

Katie needed to talk with Daniel. Alone. She stood and walked to the railing, glancing out over the ocean. "I can't get over how beautiful it is here. Thank you both for your hospitality."

"Bella, you're not a guest, this is your home," Anthony said, setting the photo album on the table.

She turned to face them and forced a smile. "If

you'll excuse us, Daniel and I would like to take a walk along the beach before heading to bed."

"It's dark," Giovanni argued.

"Not with the moon and the patio lights." Katie sent a pleading glance to Anthony.

He waved over Lorenzo. "Accompany them."

"That's not necessary," Katie insisted.

"It's always necessary," Giovanni retorted.

"Bella, Lorenzo will keep a respectable distance to allow you privacy, but your security is of utmost concern." Anthony nodded at his bodyguard. "Have Zach join us and keep watch from here."

Lorenzo pulled out his cell phone and made a call. Within seconds, the younger bodyguard appeared from the house, palming his weapon.

"Tell me again how we're not prisoners." Katie stormed toward the slate steps, Daniel at her side.

"It's for your own good," Anthony called. "Mr. Knight, I'll warn you only once. Don't try anything stupid."

The sand restricted her pace, and she didn't speak until they'd reached the shore. She slowed, keeping out of the ocean's grasp and peered over her shoulder. Lorenzo followed but true to Anthony's promise, stayed several feet away. She prayed her performance and the crashing waves would keep the Marinos away while drowning out her voice.

Katie tucked her arm through the crook of Daniel's and whispered, "We need to talk."

Daniel eyeballed Lorenzo. The bodyguard wasn't within hearing distance—provided they spoke quietly—however, he was within shooting distance so an attempted escape wasn't wise.

Katie stayed close to him, her stride determined.

"What's on your mind?" he whispered.

"Anthony clammed up in Giovanni's presence. He's adamant about finding—"

"Garrett's instructions were clear," Daniel interrupted. The mention of his mentor's omission grated on him, but he wouldn't allow himself to dwell on the matter. Garrett had his reasons for not sharing the information with Daniel. "There's more to Marino's inquiry than a missing family heirloom."

"Are Giovanni and my father telling the truth about my mother?"

My father. Two words that set Daniel's worry into overdrive. Was she wearing down? Had she started accepting Anthony? "Garrett always said the best lies were laced with truth. There's some truth to the things they mentioned about Garrett and your mother's situation."

"Situation?" Katie tilted her head.

"Garrett loved Evangelina and wanted to marry her."

"They never behaved like anything other than siblings."

"I don't think his feelings were reciprocated. I wish I could give you all the answers but I can't. Just..."

"What?"

"Don't believe everything the Marinos say—they're professional con men."

"I know." She stopped and rocked back on her heels. "Should I use the safe Anthony offered?"

Daniel considered that option. "He might be setting you up." If so, why not take the locket? Marino had proven he wasn't above breaking the law to get what he wanted.

"Do you think they know about the numbers?" Katie furrowed her brows, keeping close to his side.

"That's a definite probability. And it explains why they're playing up the family thing. Right now, it's our only bargaining tool. Once they get what they want, they'll eliminate both of us."

"Mama and Garrett are dead. They can't offer any defense. It's one person's word against another. I'm caught in the middle." Katie released her hold and threw up her hands as if to say, *I give up.*

"Katie, you're the strongest woman I know. Whatever the truth is, we'll figure it out together."

"Thank you." She smiled, tucking her arm into his.

They strode along the water's edge, enjoying the scenery and the company. Minus Lorenzo.

"What was the deal with Tiffany?" Katie's question sounded innocent enough.

Daniel detected an unspoken something. He wasn't sure exactly what, but a part of him hoped it was jealousy. Or at least, interest. "She's different."

"She's really pretty."

Ah, so that's it. Tiffany's little attempt at dissuasion hadn't gone unnoticed. "I guess. Although she's not my type." Daniel caught a glimpse of Katie's grin.

"Really? What's your type?"

"Let's just say the bar's been forever raised on my idea of the perfect woman." *Since you came into my life.* Because no one compared to Katie.

"Funny, because my taste has recently evolved."

"Do tell."

"I'm finding the rugged, lawman type to be intriguing."

"Hm. Good to know."

They stood at the water's edge as it crashed in a steady, rhythmic pattern, contrasting Daniel's rapid pulse. He guided Katie, keeping her back to Lorenzo.

Daniel shifted uncomfortably. He needed to get honest with her. She deserved his transparency.

"I have something to tell you. Giovanni and I had quite the conversation. He offered to help me find my sister if I agreed to leave."

"Oh." Katie blinked, withdrawing her arm from his hold and spun on her heel. She walked away, facing the ocean. Her words were barely audible. "I understand if you need to go."

Daniel ignored the voice in his head telling him to stay professional. He moved behind her, placing his hands on her shoulders.

She didn't resist his touch.

"I won't pretend that I didn't think over his offer. Five years of searching for Brittany with no results has been hard on my family."

Katie turned, a shimmer of tears reflected in the dim moonlight. She averted her gaze and bit her lip.

That look gave Daniel confirmation of what he'd known since he met her. Katie had his commitment. She was vulnerable and he wouldn't allow the Marino monsters to hurt her. He stepped closer, gently tilting her head to face him. "The problem is, I have this horrible propensity to be stubborn."

"Oh, yeah?" Her smile quivered, drawing his attention to the fullness of her lips.

He struggled to swallow the beach towel in his throat. "Yep. I always finish what I start." His tone was husky and he leaned back, absorbed by her emerald eyes. "So, you're stuck with me."

Katie lifted her chin, her lips beckoning him to seal the words. "Well, I'd hate to be the one responsible for you not finishing something, especially if you're going to be chief someday."

Daniel's heart swelled at her thoughtful words, making him want to kiss her more than anything. More than his next breath. "I'm in this with you."

"Promise?"

"I promise." He lowered his head, feeling her breath warm against his skin. *Stay professional. Remember Garrett. No woman is worth losing your career over.* Daniel inhaled Katie's enticing scent, his arms trembling at the restraint required to keep him from kissing her. And for the first time in his life, he wasn't sure he believed his personal mantra. Katie Tribani was worth giving up his career. Worth giving up everything.

Katie looked down, breaking her gaze. "We should probably get back." She tucked her hands into her hoodie pocket.

Right. Get back in the game. In his peripheral, Daniel caught sight of Lorenzo inching closer. He shoved his hands into his pockets. "Our company's getting nosy."

Katie nodded and they increased their pace. When they'd gained a little more distance, backs still to Lorenzo, she spoke, "Anthony made it clear he's not going to let me leave."

Daniel gritted his teeth. "We're not asking."

"They're playing the family card, right?"

"Yeah…"

"He seems more than willing to divulge information to me outside of Giovanni's presence."

"They're going to lose patience with you if they don't get what they want. Anthony seems sweet now, but remember what I've told you about his methodology."

"I agree. Give me one day. If by tomorrow evening, we don't have any real information, we leave. Do you have a plan?"

"Sort of. Let me work on Priscilla. She's the most reasonable here. I don't need a gun to break us free, but we do need a vehicle."

Daniel would do his job and protect Katie without hesitation. He'd stay by her side until one of the Marinos grew tired of his presence, or realized the threat he posed. And he'd guess that time was quickly approaching because they were leaving tomorrow whether Katie realized it or not.

THIRTEEN

Katie's eyes flew open to darkness, and she gasped, unable to breathe. She was suffocating… dying. Desperate, she tried to push herself up, but her arms and legs were bound. A weight pressed down on her chest and mouth, smothering her screams. She thrashed her head back and forth, fighting for relief.

"Stop moving or I'll squeeze the life out of you," the man growled. "The locket isn't yours. Tell me where it is, and I might let you live."

The blindfold shifted and Katie tilted her head, struggling to see the attacker. His hand partially covered her nose, restricting her airflow. The urgent need for oxygen overrode her desire to identify him. She bucked, trying to throw him off, but he was too heavy and pinned her down.

"Keep fighting me, and you'll suffocate yourself. If you make a sound, I'll kill you. Do you understand?"

She nodded, trying to place where she'd heard his voice before.

He slowly removed his hand. "Where is the locket?"

Katie sputtered, breathless and sucking in air. Was having the locket worth this? *Daniel said it was their only bargaining tool.* "My mother never gave me a locket," she choked.

"Liar! Just like your mother!" He slapped her across the face.

Katie's head jerked to the side from the impact. Her cheek stung, and she blinked back tears. The bitter scent of cigarettes drifted to her, tickling her nose. He clamped his hands around her throat, crushing her windpipe. Just before she blacked out, he released his grip.

She coughed, frantic, needing air.

"Tell me where it is," the man growled.

Tears filled her eyes. "Please, if I could, I would give you whatever you're looking for."

"Maybe you require stronger persuasion."

Katie felt a cold object against her cheek, moving slowly down her face. He continued his perusal, and she cringed. *Please, God...don't let him...* It was now or never. She let out the loudest, ear-piercing scream she could muster.

The man cursed, and the bed bounced. His pounding footsteps faded from the room.

Katie cried louder, fear and anger surging through her body. She inhaled then exhaled a scream. Her throat was dry and scratchy, but she refused to relent and continued blaring at the top of her lungs. She thrashed, fighting against the restraints.

Heavy footsteps rushed toward her, growing louder.

Please, God, help me. She let loose again, using

every ounce of oxygen to increase the volume of her cries.

Light broke through the blindfold and hurried steps drew closer.

"Katie?" Daniel's voice. "What's going on here? It's me!"

She gasped with relief. "Daniel! Help me!"

The mattress shifted with his weight, while he worked to remove the mask from her eyes. He yanked off the bindings from her hands and feet.

Katie jerked free and scrambled off the bed. She stumbled backward against the wall, knocked over the lamp on the nightstand and stood shivering. Goose bumps covered her exposed skin and she rubbed vigorously.

Daniel approached with open arms, but she stepped out of his reach. Rejection flitted in his expression as he walked around and sat in the armchair giving her space.

Tears blurred Katie's eyes as she sulked to his side. Not wanting to be touched, yet needing him.

"What happened? Who did this?" Daniel's jaw was tight.

"I… I don't know. A man." She shivered and put a hand to her neck, gingerly touching the tender spots. The attacker's hands were gone, but the phantom sensation of him crushing her throat still lingered. Katie swallowed against the tenderness from her screams.

"Here." Daniel stood and offered a blanket from the foot of the bed.

She wasn't cold, but Katie allowed him to wrap the warmth around her shoulders. Her body's involuntary flinch at his touch caught both of them off guard. She gave him an apologetic grimace. "He demanded the locket."

"Did you tell him—"

"No," she whispered. "He said if I made a sound, he'd kill me."

"And you screamed? That was either very brave or crazy."

Daniel reached for her, and this time Katie surrendered to his embrace. "I had to. I felt something cold, like steel. A knife maybe? He started to… and I was afraid he'd… Uncle Nick always taught me that in a situation like that, scream anyway."

"Smart." Daniel's arms were strong, his scent reassuring. "Did you recognize his voice?"

Katie pushed back, regarding him. "I don't know."

"Think hard. Did he sound like anyone familiar?"

She forced herself to remember the words the attacker had spoken, nibbling on a fingernail. "Possibly? Sort of like the creepy guy I headbutted at the ranch house. He smelled like cigarettes too." Katie gasped, covering her mouth, and dropped onto the bed. "It was him!"

"Had to be working for Giovanni then. I should never have left you."

For a moment, she agreed. "How *did* you hear me? Your room's so far away."

Daniel's words tumbled out like a teenager caught after curfew. "I heard footsteps in the hallway. When I opened the door, there was no one around. Figured I'd check things out, maybe find my gun while I had the chance. I'd just put on my boots when I heard you scream."

Was he lying to her too? Did he plan on leaving her to find his sister? Katie lifted a brow. "Did you see a man running out of my room?"

"No. I heard you, then someone running and your door was open."

Daniel promised to stay with her. She needed to remember that. To remember their time on the beach. Doubting him wasn't the way to handle this.

Katie looked down, inspecting her wrists. The red welts were remnants from the white strips of cloth that hung from the headboard and footboard. "Anthony said Giovanni would do anything to get that locket. Guess he wasn't exaggerating." Her voice was hoarse.

"Bella, is everything all right?" Anthony stood in the doorway, dressed in a black robe and slippers. Concern etched his face.

How long had he been there?

"Someone attacked her," Daniel snapped.

Katie pulled the blankets tighter over her shoulders as Anthony rushed to her side. Daniel blocked his way, forcing the man to go around him. The protective gesture touched her.

"Are you hurt?" Anthony sat next to her, lifting his frail hand to brush a stray lock of hair from her face.

Katie retracted from Anthony's touch. "A little."

"Can you not see she's hurt? Look at her," Daniel barked.

Anthony frowned, folding his hands in his lap.

"She's been in danger from the moment you reentered her life." Daniel's rigid stance and fisted hands demonstrated a defensive pose. "She could've been killed tonight. The bruises on her neck and cheek are already forming. We need to go to a hospital and have her checked out."

Anthony turned to him, the apprehension in his expression hardened into resolve. "Mr. Knight, please close the door."

A long pause and without words, Daniel complied.

"Bella, do you remember what I said about the locket?"

"Yes." Katie nodded. "But I don't—"

"Giovanni believes your mother gave the locket to you. I fear he may become more aggressive," Anthony warned.

"More aggressive? You know she's in danger, yet you refuse to let us go. Where was your faithful Lorenzo when all of this happened? Shouldn't he be protecting Katie instead of guarding us like we're the enemy?" Daniel's low snarl kept Katie on edge. "Giovanni's the one behind this."

"Do you think it's that easy?" Anthony bit back. "He is my son. And he is dangerous. I'm an old man. I don't know which of my men are faithful to me, and which are faithful to Giovanni."

"Do you have hidden security cameras? Maybe some right here in Katie's room?" Daniel's accusation continued, "Besides watching our every move, could one of those caught the intruder?"

"You're paranoid! You really think I'd put a camera in my daughter's room?" Anthony turned to Katie. "The only cameras we have are on the parameter of the property! I will make sure Lorenzo follows up on those." He shot a venomous glare at Daniel. "We will find who did this."

"Do you believe Lorenzo is trustworthy?" Katie asked.

"I want to believe he's loyal. Money changes people." Anthony's shoulders sagged and he shook his head. "One thing you'll soon learn, my Bella, is be careful whom you trust." He turned to Daniel, emphasizing the point.

"I knew her before she had money, so she's safe with me," Daniel said, sarcasm thick.

"I don't *have* anything," Katie argued.

The wrinkles around Anthony's eyes deepened. "Perhaps it was a mistake bringing you here. In my desperation, I failed to calculate the costs." He stood, pacing between the window and bed.

"We're leaving here, now!" Daniel asserted, going to Katie's side. "Get dressed." Then to Anthony, he said, "You can provide a vehicle for us or I'll help myself to one, but we're not staying here another minute."

"You will not order me around in my home! And no one is taking my daughter from me again!" Anthony bellowed.

Katie sat up straighter, frustration building. "Excuse me. Could both of you talk to me and not about me? I'm a grown woman capable of making up my own mind."

Anthony frowned. "I'm sorry. You're right. Mr. Knight, please give me a minute alone with my daughter."

"You've got to be kidding me. There's no way I'm leaving Katie alone with anyone in this house."

She looked between the men. Anthony's pleading expression piqued her curiosity. She gave Daniel a slight nod. "It's okay."

He flexed his jaw, clearly, not in agreement. His exaggerated hesitance was obvious by his sluggish movement. "I'll be on the other side. You've got five minutes." The door slammed behind him.

Anthony faced Katie, his eyes shadowed by gray circles. "Do you trust Mr. Knight? If not, we'll have him removed immediately."

I trust Daniel with my life. And my heart. Katie

shifted her gaze, tucking the blankets under her arms. "Daniel is my friend, and I trust him implicitly. What does he have to gain by hurting me?"

"You are a wealthy woman and will be even more so when I'm dead. Perhaps he's waiting for a payout. His predecessor was a liar and a thief. What makes you think Mr. Knight's any different?"

"I know you think you have reason to hate Mason Garrett, but he was a good man. He took care of me."

"That is debatable." Anthony cleared his throat. "I will do whatever it takes to protect you."

"Then let us leave."

Anthony grasped her hands and sat down. His slacked posture and downturned lips aged him before her eyes. "Please, Bella, give me one more day. I must put some things in order before I can let you go. Twenty-four hours is all I ask. Then, if you still want to leave me, I will reluctantly agree to your wishes."

Had she heard him correctly? Katie leaned forward. "You'll let me leave?"

"Yes, if that's your desire."

"Okay."

"One other condition. Giovanni cannot know about our agreement. It's imperative that he suspects nothing. Do you understand?" Anthony's eyebrows creased.

"I understand."

He sighed and pushed himself up to a standing position. His hunched shoulders and sluggish manner revealed his frailty. Was he sorrowful at their arrangement? He opened the door and waved Daniel inside, then returned to the armchair.

Giovanni trailed in behind Daniel. "I heard what happened. Are you all right?"

Katie studied him. The man never looked frazzled or out of control. Would he reveal frustration if he'd ordered the failed attack? "I'm fine."

"Giovanni, where's Lorenzo?" Anthony interjected, shrinking under Daniel's scrutiny.

"I'm sure I don't know, Father. I'll check into it," Giovanni said in a calm, placating tone. He gestured at Daniel's boots. "It's a good thing Mr. Knight heard Bella and was able to respond so quickly. He even had time to put on his boots."

"I stepped out of my room before Katie screamed," Daniel retorted.

"Really? For what?" Giovanni asked.

"I thought I wasn't a prisoner. Do I need a reason?" Daniel narrowed his eyes, his jaw tense.

"Interesting." Giovanni gave a slight shake of his head.

Daniel focused on Giovanni. "You're the man in the know. Any idea who would want to hurt Katie?"

"It could've been anyone," Giovanni debated.

Daniel closed the distance between him and Anthony. "Anyone who happened to know this was her room? Anyone who could get past your legion of bodyguards?"

Katie slapped the bed. "Shouldn't you have someone out looking for whoever tried to kill me tonight? Or do you already know, Giovanni? Because I think I do."

His cold smile sent a chill up her spine. "Do tell, who attacked you, little sister?"

Katie wouldn't let this man intimidate her. "The same man who attacked me in Nebraska."

"Wouldn't that be one of your men?" Daniel baited.

"I'll pretend you're not accusing me and will make sure Lorenzo is reprimanded for his lack of protection." Giovanni snatched his cell phone from his belt clip and stormed into the hallway.

Daniel faced Anthony. "Give us a way to get out of here before something worse happens."

"I can't..." Anthony wrung his hands and shuffled to the doorway, peering out. He turned to face Katie. "I will order Lorenzo to stand guard."

"Try again," Daniel said.

Remembering Anthony's promise, Katie interceded, "Daniel, I'll also make sure the door is locked."

Anthony appeared pleased as he took her hand. "Please, Bella. Just a little longer. That's all I ask."

She nodded, and he glanced over his shoulder once more before exiting the room.

Daniel pushed the door closed. "What was that about?"

Katie relayed Anthony's request and his promise to release them.

"Well, his twenty-four hours started the minute they kidnapped us. Tomorrow, we're leaving, with or without his help."

She considered arguing. Having everyone boss her around was getting old. Fast. Except she agreed with Daniel. "Okay."

"Are you sure about having one of their guards outside your door? I'd sleep in the hallway if necessary."

She grinned. "I appreciate the offer, but you need rest as much as I do." Katie looked down, studying her hands.

"What's on your mind?"

"Giovanni's trying to kill me, and Anthony's terrified of him. I want to get out of here."

"We can leave now."

"No, I gave Anthony my word." Compassion tugged at her heart for the old man. She squelched it before it took hold.

"Okay…" Daniel leaned against the wall.

"You know as much as I don't want to admit it, Anthony's been nothing but kind, protective and concerned. Everything I'd hoped a father would be. We might've had a good relationship in other circumstances. Too bad the criminal side of him is the part I can't ignore."

"You scared me for a moment there. I thought you were caving."

"No. It's only sheer morbid curiosity keeping me here. When his time is up, we're out of this place. One way or the other."

Daniel walked to the door, placing his hand on the knob. "Are you sure you'll be okay in here?"

"I'm sure. Surely no one would attack me twice in a night," Katie reassured, though she doubted sleep would come again.

"Lock the door." Daniel exited the room.

Katie threw off the covers and scurried to the door, securing the lock. For added protection, she dragged over the armchair, adjusting it beneath the handle.

She climbed into the bed and slid under the covers. Daniel's absence left her lonely. Missing him. Their conversation on the beach had convinced her mind what her heart already knew. She was falling for Daniel. His promise to stay with her, even when he could leave to help his sister, said more than words ever could. But love—or whatever she felt for Daniel—wasn't selfish. He'd already made his professional ambitions clear. He deserved to get promoted and she wouldn't stand in his way.

Katie glanced at the chair blocking her bedroom door before turning off the light. Would that hold if another attempt was made on her life?

FOURTEEN

Daniel hated the sight of Lorenzo's ugly mug and the—surgically attached, since he was never without it—MP5. Not only had the jerk jolted him awake from the restless night of sleep, he'd "encouraged" Daniel to shower and change his clothes. If he hadn't caught a whiff of his sweaty two-day-old scent, Daniel would've fought more about the issue.

Twenty minutes later, he sat opposite Anthony Marino in a sunrise breakfast meeting. Lorenzo leaned against the doorway of the dining room, guarding the entrance and any possibility of an escape. A fractional part of Daniel wondered if the elaborate breakfast buffet—spanning the oversize dining room—was his last meal.

He sighed, tired of waiting for the decrepit Marino to explain why he'd been forced to attend the meeting. "Look Marino, let's not play games. Since we both know I'm not here by choice—"

"We all have choices, Mr. Knight," Anthony interrupted. He appeared tired. More than tired, worn down.

"You realize you've left Katie's room unguarded."

Anthony steepled his hands on the table. "This won't take long, and I have Zach keeping watch over her. He's capable of protecting my daughter."

Daniel clamped his mouth closed before expressing his disagreement. He wanted to finish this conversation and get back to Katie.

"I have requested your presence to discuss the options for my daughter's safety."

"Requested? I guess that's one way to describe being dragged here at gunpoint." Daniel scowled.

Anthony shook his head, either from age or annoyance. "Mr. Knight, this isn't easy to say, so please refrain from your constant urge to add unnecessary commentary and allow me to finish."

Daniel gritted his teeth and gave a quick jerk of his head.

"You know, the curious thing about lies is that too many of them are hard to control. Before long, they take on a life of their own. They're a two-edged sword, cutting both ways."

A Bible verse from Daniel's childhood floated to mind. *Great, philosophical lessons at dawn.*

Anthony continued, "Isabella's lifetime of deceit demands I set things straight before she leaves."

Leaves. The word renewed Daniel's attention. "What do you want?"

"I wasn't aware Giovanni sent men after you in Nebraska and again in Colorado."

"I gathered that yesterday. Were you aware he ordered them to kill us?"

Anthony frowned. "No. Please understand—

I only want time with my daughter before I die. I am quite disturbed at Giovanni's exuberance."

"Is that a nice way of saying attempted murder?"

Anthony's eyebrows furrowed. "I have a confidential request to make. It must be kept between you and me. Otherwise, all of our lives may be at risk."

"Does you and I include Lorenzo?" Daniel gestured toward the bodyguard.

Anthony twisted in his seat as if seeing Lorenzo for the first time. "You don't think I'd be naive enough to sit here unguarded, do you?"

Daniel narrowed his eyes. "Fine. What kind of request?"

"I fear my son's impatience in gaining his inheritance may cause him to act irrationally."

"You think Giovanni's going to try and kill you?"

"Not just me."

"Katie," Daniel murmured, making the connections in his mind. "Your men were sent to retrieve Katie. Giovanni's were sent to kill her."

Anthony nodded. "I cannot lose my daughter again."

"So, help me get Katie out of here."

"Today I will put things into place. Things I must talk with her about. For that, she needs to be present. Once I've completed those particular items, you both will be free to leave. However,

Giovanni cannot know about our arrangement or that I suspect his part in her attack. I must know she's being protected at all times."

"You'll let us go?" Daniel clarified.

Anthony met his eyes. "It breaks my heart, but I will not keep her here if it means risking her life."

"I agree. On that note, I'd appreciate a gun—preferably mine."

"In due time. For now, you must protect Isabella here and outside of my home without letting Giovanni know we've made this agreement."

"He already knows I don't trust him. No big secret there."

"Once you leave the security of my home, I want you to come under my employment. I'm sure my compensation outweighs the government's. Then we'll both be working for the same side, and I can be assured of your loyalty to me."

"The only person I'm loyal to is Katie, and I don't work for criminals."

Anthony's hands fisted in his lap. "I'm no criminal. Stop believing the slander you've heard about me woven by Mason Garrett and my insane wife." He spat the last words. "Let me ask you, do you have any personal knowledge of me and my family? Or is your belief based on what you've been told?"

Daniel barely considered the questions. "I know what the case files, evidence and my mentor, Garrett, taught me."

Anthony sighed. "Evidence? You mean the planted evidence? Then you've been conned. All I ask is you give me a fair chance. If you find me to be the criminal you believe, fine. Hate me because it's what *you* believe, not because you're blindly following like a trained monkey. Garrett and Evangelina made the perfect getaway. Blame me, turn State's evidence and run off into the sunset."

"Garrett was a good man." Daniel's weak argument didn't address Anthony's accusation. Would Garrett's love for Evangelina cause him to do those things?

"Does a good man tear a family apart? Does a good man deceive a little girl and brainwash her to believe his lies? Good men don't do those things, yet Mason Garrett did them all."

Daniel swallowed. "Let me get this straight. It's work for you or be eliminated?"

"You are free to go, Mr. Knight, without repercussions. If you're incapable of protecting her, it might be better if you left."

"I'm not leaving her."

"I know you won't. That's why I brought you here in the first place. Your strong work ethic will keep you here, even if you aren't forced." Anthony sipped his coffee. "Love is stronger than obligation."

Daniel clamped his mouth shut. What? Love? No, this was a job. Wasn't it?

Marino continued. "As for your gun, I cannot return that to you without giving away that you're under my employ. If Giovanni suspects anything, he will...react. As I said, I'll do my best to find you a weapon. In the meantime, you must use your skills as a weapon. We're on the same side. Both of us want the best for Isabella."

"Her name is Katie."

"No, she's been conditioned into taking a name that's not hers and denied her birthrights as a Marino. Don't keep her from knowing the family she's always wanted."

"And you think you know what Katie wants?" Daniel asked.

"Everyone desires love and acceptance. Use your own brain to make judgments about us before you attempt to whisk Isabella away. Don't be the mindless civil servant following government orders." Anthony's arms shook from exertion as he pushed himself to a standing position.

For a brief second, Daniel considered assisting the man.

"I ask your discretion of this conversation for all of our sakes."

"Giovanni offered to help me find my sister," Daniel blurted, surprising himself at the uncensored words.

Anthony paused. "You may take Giovanni up on his offer to leave and obtain the information about your sister. I would certainly understand if you'd prefer to do so. Family is important. However, you should also consider that Isabella is in danger. You must decide which you can devote yourself to. You cannot serve two masters."

"Why not have Lorenzo do the job for you?" Daniel glared at the bodyguard.

"Lorenzo's duties are to ensure my safety. Money makes enemies and creates friends. True devotion cannot be bought. You obviously care for Isabella. Unless you've grown a quick affection for Giovanni, I'm guessing you don't like him. Or me."

Daniel nodded. "True."

"Then you would be the one who would selflessly protect my daughter. I can be assured of that. Consider my offer."

Psychopaths were known for their charismatic abilities and no matter how genuine he played the part, Daniel wasn't buying Anthony's long-lost father adoration. Was he?

He'd seen the case files. Planted evidence. Was that possible? Had Garrett's love for Evangelina made him blind to justice? He didn't want to question Garrett's loyalty, but the tiniest seed of doubt fought to take root.

Giovanni entered, dressed in another custom-fit suit. "Good morning. I'm surprised you're up so early. What have I missed?"

"Housekeeping items. Mr. Knight and I came

to an understanding regarding his stay here." Anthony sat down again.

Giovanni pulled out a chair across from Daniel. His unbelieving gaze fixated on his father.

Between Giovanni and Anthony, it was getting harder to tell who was the bigger criminal in this bizarre family circle. Daniel recalled the flight to the Marino estate and The Professor's words about picking the winning side. What side would that be?

"Good morning, Bella."

Katie shot up in the bed, heart in her throat at the sound of Priscilla's voice. The woman smiled, perched on the edge of her bed. *Okay, that's not creepy at all.*

She blinked against the morning sunlight streaming through the window. The curtains had been tied back. How long had Priscilla been there? "What time is it?" Katie turned to look at the door. "Where's Daniel?"

The armchair had been returned to its proper location. How had she gotten in without Katie hearing?

"Early, hon. The men are already up and moving. I'm here on a private matter."

"Before coffee?" Katie pushed herself to a sitting position, hugging a pillow.

Priscilla scooted closer invading her personal space bubble. "Giovanni's behind the attack on you. When he wants something, he will do whatever it takes to get it. He has no limits. All for a stupid piece of jewelry."

Katie considered playing dumb, but she was growing weary of the effort. "How do you know about the locket?"

Priscilla tilted her head. "Everyone knows. Your father was furious when he couldn't find it. He knew Evangelina had taken the priceless item. Who could blame her? She'd endured so much."

Katie fought the urge to shake the maid or shove her off the bed. "I don't mean to be rude, but could we continue this conversation after I've gotten dressed?"

"You're in danger."

Was that the standard conversation icebreaker in this house? "Yes, I keep hearing that." Katie worked to keep the snark from her tone.

"Several billion dollars mysteriously disappeared from the Marino's accounts when Evangelina left. Truth be told, the money belonged to her, but Anthony doesn't see it that way. He believes the locket is the missing piece in retrieving that money."

Katie's heart pounded against her ribs. *The engraved numbers inside the locket were account numbers.* She feigned a yawn. "I don't understand what this has to do with me."

"Giovanni wants that money."

"He already has everything. What more could the man possibly want?"

Priscilla tsked. "Greed is a selfish, insatiable taskmaster. For Giovanni, it's not about the money, it's about Evangelina choosing you over him."

"That was two decades ago, and he's a grown man. Besides, I had nothing to do with any of Mama's choices. Whatever her reasons, she must've loved Giovanni. I can only imagine her sorrow at leaving behind her son."

"Yes, but their relationship was…different. Your mother was a wonderful lady. Kind and merciful even under the most dreadful of circumstances."

"What kind of circumstances?"

The weight of the information appeared to drain energy from Priscilla. "That's for another day." She reached for Katie's hands. "Sweet Bella, don't doubt your father's love. He's missed you and is desperate for a relationship with you. It's no secret he's done many awful things, but everyone deserves forgiveness. Anthony's time in prison made him a changed man. Don't waste your precious moments together on suspicions or being distant. Enjoy the renewed relationship for however long it lasts."

Katie forced a smile, refusing to allow her doubts about Anthony to be loosed from her heart.

"He's been generous. However, I'd be less skeptical if I weren't held prisoner here."

"He's on borrowed time." Priscilla pursed her lips. "Upon Anthony's passing, he desires that you and Giovanni share the estate. You are an obstacle to Giovanni's goals, and the locket is merely a stepping stone for him. Once he finds what he's looking for, he'll want to be rid of you."

"Because if Giovanni gets rid of me—"

"He'll inherit the entire fortune."

Katie rubbed the goose bumps from her arms, eager for Priscilla to go. "I appreciate your concern, but as I've said repeatedly, my mother never gave me a locket." Do extenuating circumstances like survival excuse lying? *Forgive me, Lord.*

Priscilla quirked an eyebrow and stood. "I see. Well, I'll let you get ready for breakfast." Before exiting the room, she said, "The men are meeting in the dining room."

Did the woman think Katie would blurt the locket's whereabouts? She threw back the covers and got up. Her gaze fell to the sneaker poking out from underneath the bed. The same shoe where she'd hidden the locket. Curious, she pressed her foot on the toe of the shoe, feeling the shift of the necklace inside. Had Priscilla found it? Is that why she was so adamant about sharing her suppositions regarding Giovanni?

Katie glanced at the door once again noticing how the chair had been moved without her hearing

Priscilla enter. A reminder that Daniel had already gone to breakfast, leaving her without protection. *Thanks a lot.*

Irritation gave her a turbo boost, fueling her to complete a shower in record time.

A brief reduction of her momentum came as she contemplated clothing options. Days in the same hoodie and pants held no appeal. The closet full of clothes—conveniently yet no less than creepy—already in her size, beckoned. Before she could talk herself out of it, Katie chose a pair of designer jeans, a purple cotton blouse and a white duster sweater that hung to her knees, covering the front pocket where she'd placed the necklace. It pressed against her leg. A pair of white gladiator sandals caught her eye, but that might encourage Anthony to believe she'd surrendered to his provision. Katie pulled on her own sneakers, hurried to the door and swung it open.

She jumped back, startled. The shorter guard she'd met the night before stood waiting inches from her in the doorway, wearing a big grin. "Good morning, Bella."

Nothing about his boyish appearance was intimidating except for the Sig Sauer perched on his hip. Could she snag the gun? Right and do what? Run through the house firing like she was in a bad Western?

"We haven't been introduced. I'm Zach. I'll escort you down to the dining hall. Mr. Knight and the Marinos are waiting for you." He reached for her arm.

Katie shifted out of his reach. "I'm good."

Zach frowned and touched the weapon reminding her who was in charge.

She pushed by, not bothering to acknowledge the man-child's eyes on her. Katie raced down the stairs. She gripped the banister railing as her shoes squeaked on the polished floor.

Zach's quick footsteps followed behind as she skidded into the dining room where Lorenzo stood, guarding the doorway. He cleared his throat and shifted, announcing her entry.

Daniel, Giovanni and Anthony sat at the expansive table, their heated discussion stalled at her arrival.

Fear turned to irritation. "I would've come earlier, had someone shared what time breakfast would be served." She didn't try to hide the sarcasm aimed at Daniel.

"I'm afraid that's my fault," Anthony defended. "I woke Daniel early to go over some security details."

The scowl on Daniel's face said otherwise.

"Really? Security for what?" Katie walked around the table toward Daniel.

"It's really something men handle. Nothing a woman should be concerned with," Giovanni said.

Katie glared, fighting back her rude reply.

Anthony rose with arms wide. “Bella, you look beautiful as always.”

Compelled to acknowledge the elder man’s extension of warmth, she shuffled toward him and stood in his awkward embrace.

“Don’t be angry—I’ll explain later,” Anthony whispered against her ear, sealing his words with a light kiss on the cheek.

His gentleness and response to her hurt feelings chipped a hole in her anger armor.

“Sit here, Katie.” Daniel pulled out the chair next to him.

Grateful for the interception, she withdrew from Anthony and slid into the seat. She grinned at Daniel’s change of clothing, noting he wore his own military-style boots. She glanced down considering her shoe choice.

Daniel’s dark blue shirt and jeans complimented him, enhancing his handsome features. The smell of soap drifted to her, confirming he’d also taken a shower. Her appreciation was sideswiped by the remembrance that he’d left her unguarded.

“Thank you,” she said dryly.

Priscilla rushed into the room and spoke as though it was their first encounter for the morning. “Good morning, Bella. Mr. Marino prefers a buffet-style breakfast so grab a plate and help yourself. If you don’t see something you’d like, let me know and I’ll have it made for you.”

Katie twisted to see an expansive table filled with food.

"She gets it," Giovanni snarled.

Priscilla's smile fell. With slumped shoulders, she hurried out of the room.

Katie glowered at him. Why was he always so cruel to the woman? She stood and walked toward the food. Eggs, sausage, bacon, pancakes, waffles, breads and muffins galore. "All of this is for us?"

Giovanni laughed. "When you're a king, you eat like one."

She ignored his arrogance and grabbed a plate, filling it with eggs, bacon and two different types of muffins. Her stomach growled as she returned to her place at the table. "Guess I'm hungrier than I thought."

She and Daniel delayed their consumption until Anthony and Giovanni joined them. Was her father limping a little? Or walking with exaggerated sluggishness? Katie tried not to stare, but something was off.

"I'll say grace." Without waiting for the men's agreement, Katie said a simple prayer of thanks. Opening her eyes, she saw Giovanni shovel in a forkful of food, while Daniel and Anthony politely withheld.

Daniel gave her a tight smile.

"Now that we're all here," Anthony began, placing his napkin on his lap.

Giovanni snapped his fingers at Tiffany, who'd

come in and rushed to his side, refilling his coffee cup while he leered.

What was his deal?

Anthony continued, "I'd hoped to do this in a more celebratory setting, but after last night's events, it's imperative we expedite matters."

Giovanni's attention reverted to his father.

"I'm sorry—am I late?" A tall man with curly gray-and-white hair wearing a wrinkled brown suit entered, carrying a briefcase.

"Edward. Your timing is perfect." Anthony gestured toward the buffet. "Please make yourself a plate and join us."

Katie's gaze shifted between each of the men. Giovanni's immaculate appearance was darkened by his troubled expression. His fake smile contrasted his narrowed eyes. A rattlesnake biding its time before an attack, he zeroed in on Edward.

The unkempt businessman returned with an overflowing plate and sat opposite Anthony. "Good morning." He faced Katie. "You must be Isabella."

Katie nodded unsure whether to correct him or not. Maybe a big *My Name Is Katie* button would help when meeting people in the Marino home.

"This is my attorney, the man I owe for making sure I didn't spend one more day in prison. He's brilliant," Anthony gushed.

"Brilliant would have gotten you out of prison twenty years earlier," Giovanni retorted.

Anthony winced as if someone had slapped him. "Edward, I've called you here because it's time to have Isabella reinstated in my will."

Giovanni coughed, sputtering juice onto the glass table. Composing himself, he turned to Anthony. "Father, don't you think that's a little premature?"

"What is there to wait for? I'm dying, and our Bella is home. Edward, make the necessary adjustments effective today. Giovanni and Bella will share the entire Marino fortune. In addition, Bella shall also be given my fifty-one percent of the businesses," Anthony announced.

"But I..." Giovanni stood, his perfect appearance marred by his reddened face and clenched fists. He cleared his throat. "No disrespect, but I've been managing the companies. What does she know about it? Perhaps a sixty-forty split would be a better choice."

Katie clung to her fork. It wasn't as if she wanted the authority, but Giovanni's disapproval was a little more than telling. What could she say? She didn't even know what their business dealings involved.

"Giovanni, you've proven to be an effective businessman. However, this is my decision, and it's final." Anthony sipped from his coffee cup.

"I'll have it ready for your signature before lunch." Edward reached into his jacket and withdrew his phone.

The silence hung around the group heavier than the chandeliers.

The only one who didn't appear affected by the news was Edward. He tapped away on his smartphone, then dropped the device into his pocket.

Katie stared at the table, tumultuous thoughts bouncing in her brain. Had Anthony just tossed down another gauntlet? He'd given her business authority, whatever that meant. If Marino Industries was a legitimate business—which was doubtful—or a criminal empire, did he seriously expect her to stay and run the company? Anthony's sly move contradicted his promise to let them leave.

Edward's obnoxious chewing resumed as he forked food from the mountain on his plate.

Giovanni broke the silence, pacing near his seat. "Father, may I speak with you in private?"

"We're done with secrets in this family. If you have something to say, do so now." Anthony's complexion paled, and he dropped the coffee cup, clutching the table.

"Are you okay?" Katie pushed back her chair.

Anthony rose slowly. "Forgive me. I need to lie down. Edward, have the forms completed this morning. I may be dead before tomorrow."

FIFTEEN

Katie gripped the table as Giovanni rushed to Anthony's side. He placed his hand against the elder Marino's back, steadying him. "Here, Father, hold on to me. I've got you."

Anthony's hand shook as he gripped Giovanni's shoulder. The patriarch's eyes, so similar to Katie's, glistened with moisture. "*Grazie*, my beloved son."

"You're welcome, Father," Giovanni cooed.

Their heated conversation only seconds before evaporated in concern and love as Giovanni assisted Anthony out of the dining room. The exchange only served to emphasize the bond between father and son, leaving Katie once again on the outside looking in.

She should be helping Anthony too, but she couldn't move. Memories assaulted Katie from every direction. All of those precious last days with Mama, helping with her medications, bathing and eating. They filled every waking second with vocal reminders of how much they loved one another. The vivid recollections bolted Katie's feet to the ground, constricting her throat with emotion. She clung to the tabletop watching Anthony and Giovanni, but only saw herself with Mama.

Lorenzo shifted slightly allowing the father and

son to pass while uncomfortable silence hung in the air.

Daniel's light touch snapped her into reality, releasing her from the immobile state. "Katie, are you okay?"

Her eyes blurred with memory tears and she struggled to swallow. "All I could see was me and my mother."

She shook her head, blinking away the moisture and sat. Katie lifted her fork, desperate to give her hands something to do.

Stoic as ever, Lorenzo maintained his rigid posture and expressionless face.

Edward reclined and used his fingernail to pick at his teeth. He let out a lengthy belch before slapping his palms on the tabletop. "Well, that was tasty. I'll get busy on the paperwork. Glad you made it home safely, Isabella. Talk with you soon." He shook Daniel's hand and strode out of the room whistling.

"He was interesting." Katie faced Daniel. "Why didn't you come get me this morning?"

Daniel took her hand, meeting her eyes. His touch instantly dissolved her anger and ignited her pulse. "Believe me, it wasn't my idea to come down to breakfast without you. Lorenzo and his weapon are persuasive."

"Oh." She moved food around on her plate. "Why would Anthony give me fifty-one percent of the holdings?" Giovanni was furious. "If we hadn't been here..." She shuddered and whispered, "Anthony's weak and fragile. Not to mention terrified of his own son."

Daniel frowned. "The Marinos are dangerous. They don't own the local store. They're drug runners. Crime lords."

Katie's gaze shifted to Lorenzo. Had he overheard Daniel? Anthony seemed anything but dangerous. "His illness appears to be getting worse." She considered Priscilla's words. "I can't help but wonder if he's sincere about wanting a relationship with me. Or..." She let the unspoken words linger.

"Remember what I've told you. The business transfer is another manipulation technique to keep you here."

"Right." Katie mentally slapped herself back to reality.

"Anthony can appoint you to whatever position he wants. It doesn't mean you have to accept the job of overseeing their nefarious dealings."

"What was going on when I walked in? What was the discussion really about?"

"Before we get into that, there's something you need to know." Daniel leaned closer to Katie and turned away from Lorenzo. He whispered, "Your father offered me employment to be your bodyguard—unofficially—because he doesn't trust Giovanni."

"Did you agree?"

Daniel shook his head. "You know I can't do that."

Katie bit her lip. Confirmation of everything Priscilla had told her was evident in Daniel's words. Images of the feeble and ailing Anthony added to the fear slithering up her spine. She continued the whispered conversation, mimicking Daniel's posture. "If Giovanni gets rid of you and me, he'll go after Anthony next."

Daniel shifted in his seat. "Probably."

"I apologize for my outburst." Giovanni entered the room.

"Is Anthony all right?" Katie shifted nervously in the chair.

"Yes, he needs to rest. Worked himself up with all that nonsense about the business." Giovanni returned to his seat. "Marino Industries is very lucrative. I would hate to burden you with the daily decisions that need to be made to keep it running smoothly."

Perfect lead-in for her question. "What exactly does Marino Industries do?"

"We're a successful importing and exporting company—" Giovanni sipped his coffee.

"Like guns, women and drugs?" Daniel interjected.

Giovanni slowly set down his coffee cup, glaring at Daniel. "Mr. Knight, do you ever tire of attacking our family?"

Daniel shrugged. "Just thought I'd help answer the question since you left it so open-ended."

"When the time comes, I'd be happy to sit with

you, *Isabella*, and go over the details," Giovanni emphasized her name and held her gaze. "However, we have more pressing things to discuss. I'm afraid I must burden you more."

"With what?" Katie asked.

"Father is very ill."

She placed her hands in her lap. "I think that's obvious."

"More than physically. Unfortunately, our family is cursed with mental disorders."

Daniel tapped her foot, a reminder to beware of Giovanni's lies. "I don't understand," Katie said.

"He's mild-mannered in front of company, and right now, you're still company. I'm not sure what he's told you up to this point. No doubt he's woven a tale about a priceless locket, and me wanting to take it from you." Giovanni leaned forward, his dark eyes drilling into hers.

Katie wiped her palms on her pants, grazing the necklace in her pocket. She looked past Giovanni to where Lorenzo stood. Did the guy ever take a break? Who was he loyal to—Anthony or Giovanni—or was he working for himself? The Marino house had far too many enemies and not enough allies.

"He's been obsessed with that ridiculous locket since Mother took it from him. He's not well, Isabella." Giovanni turned to face Daniel. "You're a problem."

"I beg your pardon," Daniel replied.

"Father is insanely jealous and won't share his children's affections. He also likes to keep us pitted against each other. Ever heard the saying, find a common enemy? Why do you think I'm here without a wife and children?" Giovanni placed his napkin over his empty plate, steepling his fingers.

Her brother's words dipped into Katie's well of reservations. Would Anthony really do what Giovanni accused? Is that why he offered her the chance to escape? Still, her brother was a good-looking man. Tall, physically fit and always the picture of perfection. No doubt he could have any woman he wanted.

"Please explain." Katie busied herself lifting the crystal pitcher filled with ice water and poured herself a glass.

A shadow passed over Giovanni's face. "I was in love once. She died mysteriously in a boating accident."

"You think Anthony murdered her?" Daniel pressed.

"Yes." Giovanni placed his palms on the table and rose. "Isabella, you need to send Daniel away for his own safety."

Daniel shook his head. "Let me simplify this. No one is sending me anywhere unless Katie goes with me."

"Then you might have the same fate as my beloved." Giovanni addressed Katie, "Father will rid you of everything. It's part of the reason I fought for you not to have the business ties. Once you're in this family, there's no escaping. He'll own you. Daniel, you pose a risk to Bella by being here. Father will have you removed, one way or the other."

"Is that what the big discussion was about when I walked in?" Katie asked.

Daniel nodded. "Giovanni encouraged me to leave and vouch to the authorities that there is no lawlessness happening here. To eliminate any incorrect assumptions that you've been kidnapped—"

"Which I was—" Katie said, annoyance building.

"Exactly. They don't want any heat." Daniel sat up straighter.

"Daniel will return and tell the authorities there's nothing illegal going on—" Giovanni pressed.

"You want him to lie and say everything is roses and rainbows?" Katie clarified.

"You got it." Daniel's jaw was tight.

"It's a way to get him safely out of the picture before something terrible happens," Giovanni urged.

Katie jerked to look at him, astounded at the threat. There was no way he would allow Daniel to leave that easily. Her heart drummed in her chest. They had to get out of here and fast. Her words tumbled out. "What if I return with Daniel? Wouldn't that make the most sense? They'd see I wasn't being held prisoner."

"I'm afraid that's not a possibility." Giovanni shook his head.

"Why not?" Katie asked.

Giovanni strode around the table and perched next to Katie, invading her comfort zone. "It's not safe for us to talk here," he whispered, giving a slight jerk of his head toward the doors where Lorenzo stood. "Let me arrange for an excursion on my boat. We can speak freely without worry of being overheard."

Daniel's expression clouded. "You can't be serious."

Katie stiffened.

"Mr. Knight, I'm not going to take you to the ocean to dump your body. Quit being so paranoid." Giovanni brushed an imaginary piece of lint from his pants and smoothed down his jacket.

Priscilla hurried into the room. "Mr. Giovanni, your father is asking for you and Lorenzo."

Katie felt a tiny twinge of jealousy that Anthony hadn't asked for her too.

"Excuse me." Giovanni stood. "Lorenzo, please have Zach assume your post."

"We don't need a babysitter. I want time to talk with Katie about her options. In private," Daniel inserted.

"The security is for your own safety. You may speak with Bella in this room," Giovanni said.

"You said we're not prisoners," Katie challenged.

Lorenzo moved from Katie's sight. Zach took his place wearing that boyish grin.

"We'll be right back." Giovanni exited the room.

Katie caught a glimpse of Daniel out of the corner of her eye. His taut facial muscles, narrowed eyes and fisted hands warned he was about to make a move.

It was time to get out of the Marino house. Daniel surveyed Zach—the guard he'd nicknamed the leprechaun—who stood at the doorway watching Katie like a teenager at a high school dance. *Dream on, kiddo.*

Daniel rose, Katie following as he made his way toward Zach.

The kid stood taller, hand positioned on the Sig Sauer at his hip.

"Zach?" Katie moved in front of Daniel. "We need a moment. Could you please get Tiffany to bring us a new carafe of coffee?"

He blinked. "I can't leave my post."

"Too bad." Daniel swept Zach into a choke hold before the inexperienced delinquent could grab his gun.

Katie slid the Sig out of Zach's holster.

"I don't want to hurt you. Help us get out of here and we all walk away." Daniel shifted his weight so he was behind Zach.

“They’ll kill you,” Zach rasped. “Then they’ll kill me for helping you.”

“I think that’s a reality regardless,” Katie replied.

Daniel’s grip around the kid’s neck prevented him from screaming for help. He delivered a strike to the side of Zach’s neck—a classic brachial stun—knocking him unconscious, and set the young man on the floor.

With a hurried clip through the hallway, Katie and Daniel made their way through the foyer to the entry. Katie searched the area, covering Daniel with the gun.

Something wasn’t right and quite frankly, this was too easy, but they had to take the chance.

“It’s like everyone disappeared,” Katie whispered.

Daniel peered through the window; seeing no one, he flung the door open. “Go.”

The warm sunlight greeted them as they ran to the massive six-car garage on the right of the L-shaped house. A ten-foot black iron fence surrounded the property with the gate swung wide.

“Give me the gun and look for keys hanging in any of the ignitions,” Daniel said.

Two of the garage doors were open, revealing a classic foreign convertible and black SUV. *Outstanding. Getaway car approved.*

Daniel signaled for Katie to follow him and they made their way inside. The garage was beyond impressive and resembled a showroom displaying the spotless, stunning vehicles. The other four garage doors were closed concealing a pickup truck, sports car and four-door sedan. Daniel ran to the convertible, but the keys weren't in the ignition. He moved toward the SUV while Katie checked the sedan and sports car.

The shimmer of the keys in the SUV's ignition increased his pulse. "Yes! This one!" He waved Katie over.

They jumped into the vehicle and Daniel locked the doors. He turned the key as four familiar men advanced from the house.

Daniel tried again. The SUV didn't even sputter.

"You're wasting your time." The tobacco-scented assailant from the ranch walked around to the driver's side and tapped the window with a Sig Sauer.

"Daniel, what do we do?" Katie slid closer to him.

"Get down." Daniel aimed the gun and pulled the trigger. It clicked. Empty.

"We knew you'd take down Zach. No point in wasting bullets on the kid," Giovanni called.

"I think they're trying to leave without saying goodbye." The Professor stood next to Katie's door.

A cold chill oozed through Daniel's veins. "Guess the winning side wasn't Anthony," he mumbled.

The Professor also held a Sig Sauer. Did Marino buy those in bulk for his minions?

"Get out of the SUV." Giovanni blocked the entrance, holding Daniel's Glock 21SF.

"Nice gun," Daniel growled.

Lorenzo covered the right side of the garage with his ever-present MP5.

Daniel weighed the risks, glancing between each of the armed men. His empty Sig Sauer paled in comparison to their loaded weapons. The men could hear them. *Creative instructions, coming up.* "We're in the same position as we were at the ranch, Katie."

She faced him, understanding in her eyes. "It does look that way."

"Stop wasting our time," Giovanni goaded.

"Probably get the same results," Daniel hinted.

Katie nodded. "That'd be a shame."

The tobacco-smelling assailant reached for the driver's door handle. "Get out—"

Daniel thrust open his door, smacking the man. He lunged from his seat and tackled the assailant to the ground. Daniel finished the assault by slamming the butt of his empty gun against the man's head.

Katie shrieked on the other side of the SUV.

He turned as Lorenzo's fist delivered a blindsiding punch. Daniel fell back against the vehicle. In a quick recovery, he jumped up, landing two swift blows that sent Lorenzo's aviator glasses flying.

The racking of a gun held Daniel in place.

His heart jackhammered. He had nowhere to run.

Giovanni shook his head. "I told Lorenzo if we gave you even an inch, you'd throw our hospitality in our faces and try to escape."

Lorenzo's face was beet red, and his aviator sunglasses lay broken on the ground. A thick scar ran from his right eyebrow, over his eyelid, ending under the glass eye that stared blankly past Daniel. He rubbed his jaw and leveled the MP5, silently reinforcing Giovanni's authority.

Daniel gritted his teeth.

Katie stood in front of The Professor. He held his gun against her head. "You're outnumbered—give it up."

Daniel met her eyes. They'd go down fighting.

Katie whipped her head back, connecting with The Professor's chin, then drove her elbow into his stomach. He lost hold of his gun, which clattered to the cement floor. She delivered a strike to his knee, dropping the man, and finished him with a kick to the head.

Giovanni gaped at the scene, giving Daniel the opening he needed. He charged, driving the man to the ground, and managed to land several punches to his model-perfect face. Lorenzo yanked Daniel off Giovanni and the force had him stumbling backward. Giovanni scurried and stood, chest heaving. He swiped at his bleeding nose, baring his teeth like a caged animal.

An unexpected blow to the back of his head dropped Daniel to his knees. He glared up at the tobacco-scented man standing over him, gun poised.

Lorenzo dragged Katie over to Giovanni by her hair.

Giovanni's hand shook as he pointed the gun at Katie's forehead. "We're done playing games. Take care of Mr. Knight, but keep him alive. For now. My sister and I have some unfinished business."

The Professor dragged himself up from the ground. "Well played, little girl."

Gun trained on Daniel, The Professor and the tobacco assailant approached with sneers painted on their faces.

Daniel stood and prepared for the attack. Both men moved toward him. Katie and Giovanni were behind him.

The tobacco assailant sprang first, but Daniel dodged his effort, then clocked the man. The Professor followed up with a straight punch to his stomach, taking the wind out of Daniel's lungs.

Daniel responded with an uppercut to The Professor's jaw. The other assailant kicked Daniel in the kidneys, causing his back to spasm.

The Professor attacked from behind, driving Daniel to the ground. *Move, Knight. Keep fighting.*

Daniel reared up, but The Professor slammed his face into the hot pavement. Electric streaks of pain shot through his nose, and his eyes watered. A warm, thick copper taste filled his mouth.

Lorenzo stalked the battle in a slow and steady way, his mouth curved.

"Stop," Katie cried from somewhere nearby.

Her voice jolted Daniel back into the fight. He thrust back his elbow, contacting The Professor's face. The man fell backward, hands covering his nose.

Daniel spun like a turtle on its back into the ground defense position, swinging out his legs and striking Lorenzo's knee. The man cursed and stumbled to the side, clutching his injured leg.

The tobacco man's boot slammed into Daniel's ribs, sending him reeling. The shock immobilized him long enough to give the goon a chance to kick him again. Daniel gasped for air as his ribs exploded in pain. He rolled protectively to his side, attempting to slide away from the boot's range.

The Professor pounced, jerking Daniel's arms behind his back. He couldn't restrain his cry of agony.

Lorenzo landed several punches to Daniel's face, and the world spun as he fought to stay conscious throughout the assault.

"I've been waiting for this opportunity, Marshal Man." Lorenzo winced, shifting his weight to one leg as he secured flexicuffs on Daniel's wrists. "Let's kill them now."

"Not yet," Giovanni answered.

Daniel worked his jaw, thankful it wasn't broken. He met Lorenzo's icy glare through his blurred vision. "It only took…three of you…to take me down," he replied between painful inhales around the injured rib.

"You shouldn't antagonize Lorenzo. He's got a very bad temper." Giovanni dragged Katie toward the truck.

Daniel contained the urge to shout in pain, gritting his teeth while every part of his body protested in suffering.

"Take him to the cell," Lorenzo ordered.

The Professor rasped into his ear, "A shame, you weren't smart enough to spot the winning side."

SIXTEEN

Katie's anger and adrenaline whirled through her body with tornado force. Giovanni pressed the gun into her back, shoving her toward the pickup. The Professor and the other assailant hauled Daniel away like a rodeo calf.

"Why are you doing this?"

Giovanni chuckled. "You'll understand soon."

"What do you want?"

"Little sister, you don't *have* anything I want."

"The locket. I can give you the locket."

"I could care less about some worthless piece of jewelry. You should've used that bargaining tool with Father."

Katie's head spun. Now what?

"Do what I say or you'll never see your boyfriend again. Do you understand?" Giovanni's glare pinned her through eyes so black they blended with his pupils.

She shivered.

Lorenzo stormed to them, clutching the MP5. "Now, can I kill her?"

"Patience." Giovanni chortled.

Katie startled at Lorenzo's appearance, sans aviator sunglasses. He shot her a glare and she averted her eyes, wildly surveying the area.

She could run. As if sensing her internal debate,

Lorenzo poked her back with the gun, a vivid reminder she couldn't outrun bullets.

"He's so impatient." Giovanni gripped her arm, and yanked her toward the gleaming pickup truck.

The spotless vehicle symbolized everything Giovanni represented. He'd do whatever it took to get what he wanted and look good doing it. An idea sprouted. The truck was strong. Could plow through anything. At least she hoped so.

Giovanni opened the passenger door. "Lorenzo, grab the duct tape and open the garage door."

Lorenzo hit a button on a control panel at the far wall where a row of cabinets hung. He returned with a roll of silver tape.

"Don't do this," Katie pleaded, fighting the tears that choked her words.

"Secure her," Giovanni ordered.

Lorenzo wrenched her arms forward, wrapping them with the tape.

"Make sure Mr. Knight is taken care of." Giovanni turned to Katie. "Get in."

The vehicle was lifted and with her bound hands, she struggled to obey. "I can't climb with my arms tied together."

Giovanni gripped her upper arm. "Use the running board. Are you really that dense?" He hefted her into the seat and slammed the door shut.

Her arm stung from his rough treatment. What would happen to Daniel? She had to get help.

Giovanni spoke with Lorenzo outside the vehicle. *Now.* She had to move now.

The sun cast a flicker of light off the keys dangling from the ignition. As Giovanni walked around to the driver's side, Katie hit the door locks and slid across the seat.

Lorenzo's face appeared at the passenger door window. He clung to the door handle. "Open the door before I shoot you."

Katie's hands trembled as she struggled to grasp the ignition key and turn it. The engine roared to life, and she tugged on the gear shift, successfully sliding into Drive. She stomped on the gas pedal, and the vehicle lurched into motion.

Lorenzo jumped off the side, disappearing from view.

"Stop her!" Giovanni waved his arms, running beside the vehicle.

Lorenzo stood at the gate's closed entrance with the MP5 aimed at her.

A rapid succession of gunfire and a cloud of dust from the driveway flew up in front of the pickup's grill.

Katie accelerated and ducked down in the seat. Lorenzo stayed planted in front of the gate, directly in front of her, gun leveled.

Giovanni ran toward Lorenzo. "Don't shoot my truck!"

The iron fence drew closer; she gripped the steering wheel as the engine roared.

"She's going through! Hit the spikes!" Giovanni screeched.

The steady rise of iron teeth emerged from the other side of the gate.

I can outrun them. Katie barreled through the fortress as high-pitched metal screeched mimicking a thousand fingernails on a chalkboard. The tires smashed on the spikes, resulting in a steering battle for control. She clung to the wheel, desperate to keep the vehicle from rolling as the truck swerved on the road.

Katie kept her foot pressed on the accelerator, but the pickup slowed on the rapidly deflating tires.

"No!" She pounded her bound wrists on the steering wheel. "Go, you stupid hunk of metal!"

The vehicle ignored her, as the flattened tires screeched unevenly to a pathetic crawl. Katie spotted a thick tree line bordering the road. Slamming on the brakes, she leaped from the still moving vehicle, and tumbled onto the asphalt. She cringed at the stinging pain in her ankle while forcing herself to a standing position. Katie ran with wild abandon toward the vegetation cover.

Tires squealed behind her, but she refused to look back. Wood ricocheted off a tree next to her head. Katie screamed, dodging to the side. The soft, sandy ground acted like quicksand, hindering her pace, and the sweltering humidity engulfed her lungs.

"Get her!" Giovanni's enraged voice commanded.

The thick tree line filled with leafy bushes and plants scratched at her face and body. Just when she found cover it ended, feeding into an open area. She turned to see Giovanni and Lorenzo barreling after her, covering too much ground, too fast.

She had no place to hide.

The highway splayed wide before her with no cars traveling in either direction. Giovanni's four-door sedan beckoned from several hundred feet away. Could she make it to the car? What other options did she have?

Skirting through the foliage, Katie dashed toward the vehicle.

So close. She could do this. Her feet pounded the blacktop with her desperation.

She didn't look back, but she had no doubt Giovanni and Lorenzo were chasing her. *Let's hope years of high school track and cross-country pay off.*

Katie's bound arms didn't help her momentum. She lengthened her stride, closing the distance.

The car's dark-tinted windows secreted the passenger until it was too late. The driver's door flew open, and The Professor stepped out. "Hello, Isabella."

Katie crashed into the imaginary barrier between her and the man. Before a word escaped her lips, she was tackled from behind. An *oomph* escaped her lips as she skidded on her chest, forcing the air from her lungs. Her chin, knees and arms stung from where she was sure road rash covered her bare flesh. Heat radiated from the blacktop, sweltering her body. The man's crushing weight pinned her to the ground and kept Katie from inhaling.

Lorenzo's voice reached like a claw around her throat. "You're really starting to make me mad." He stood and wrenched her upright.

Giovanni hurried over, a murderous glare carved on his face, and Daniel's Glock 21SF in his hand. The same gun Uncle Nick—Garrett—always carried.

The men shoved her into the backseat of the sedan. Wasn't it pure irony that the hoped method of escape now imprisoned her?

The air conditioning blew hard on her face where sweat trickled from her hairline. Her arms and chest burned from the torn skin.

Giovanni slid next to her, thrusting his cell phone into her face. "Little sister, you're gutsy. And stupid. Must have inherited that from our mother. I hope your little heroic stunt was worth this."

She withered in the seat, focused on the screen. Daniel sat strapped to a chair, his face badly beaten.

Katie gasped. "You're a monster."

Giovanni grinned and slid the phone into his

pocket. He leaned back as Lorenzo entered the passenger seat. The Professor climbed into the driver's seat and they sped in the opposite direction, toward the Marino home.

Confusion swarmed Katie. Why were they going back?

As if sensing her question, Giovanni said, "You ruined my truck, so we're going back for a new ride. Then we'll be on our way. Just you and me, little sister."

Lorenzo tossed back a roll of duct tape.

"You've delayed my plans, but you won't stop them." Giovanni ripped off a piece of the tape, slapping it over her mouth.

The drive back to the estate was the longest and shortest of Katie's life.

Daniel drifted back to consciousness somewhere between the beating in the garage and the musty cement storage room where he sat. He had no way of knowing how long he'd been here; based upon the aches of his muscles, he'd guess a good while.

He was restrained in a wooden chair, alone with Lorenzo, beneath a single bulb swinging from the ceiling. Classic interrogation scene.

"I figured for a marshal, you'd be smarter." Lorenzo gave Daniel an open-handed smack upside his head.

The impact sent another voltage through Daniel's aching brain. Stress breathing kept him from displaying any outward reaction. Sarcasm helped too. "Glad to see you found new sunglasses. How's the knee?"

Lorenzo shot him a murderous glare and shifted. "You'll have to do better than that to beat me."

Daniel licked his split lip—convinced he'd lost a tooth in the battle—and blinked the one eye that hadn't swollen shut. "Anthony trusts you."

Lorenzo leaned against the cement wall, chomping on a piece of red licorice. "Anthony's an old fool. I heard what he said earlier. He knows no one has real devotion to him." He laughed. "Although in this case, he was wrong. My devotion is always up for sale. Giovanni's got control of the money, and Anthony's got one foot in his coffin. Surprised you didn't accept either of their offers. Would've saved you the beating."

"Guess I'm not as easily bought and paid for as you." Maybe taunting the beast wasn't the smartest thing, but his frustration was outweighing his intelligence.

"Big words from the beaten man strapped to a chair."

Touché. Bound by flex-cuffs, Daniel's arms were secured behind his back, and his ankles were bound to the legs of the chair. He was immobile—for the moment—but continued to work against the restraints. The burning on his wrists confirmed he'd rubbed off flesh trying to free himself. His boots provided protection for his ankles. It was time for Plan B.

"Stop trying to be the hero. Your girlfriend's dead or will be soon. Giovanni will return to finish you."

Daniel slid his fingers along the chair's spindles. "Why don't you do it for him? Or is he the one calling the shots? You're the middle man? The lackey?"

Lorenzo chuckled. "Save your cop talk for someone else. I'll be whatever Giovanni needs so long as I'm kept on the payroll. And it's a good payroll."

"Now see, I would've thought you were smarter than to trust someone willing to betray his own blood. What makes you think Giovanni won't kill you once he's gotten what he wants?" Daniel watched as his words sorted through Lorenzo's oversize empty noggin.

His smile faded, replaced by the downward turn of his lips.

Score. Daniel had struck a chord.

Lorenzo snorted. "Whatever, Marshal Man." He set the MP5 on the ground and shoved his meaty paw into the licorice package, pulling out another piece. He dropped one and squatted to pick it up.

Daniel seized the opportunity. He rocked forward, lifting the chair an inch off the ground.

With a jerk, he swung the chair around, splintering the wood on Lorenzo's unsuspecting body. The flex-cuffs on his ankles broke off the demolished seat. Daniel yanked his right arm free, ripping the rest of the flex-cuffs and snatched the gun. Lorenzo stumbled upright as Daniel delivered a roundhouse kick to his head, knocking him unconscious.

The door opened and Daniel tensed, prepared to take on another of Marino's minions.

No. It couldn't be.

Priscilla's gentle eyes and softened features peeked into the room. She glanced down where Lorenzo lay sprawled on the cement floor and grinned. Stepping inside, she pushed the door closed, and clasped her hands in front of her traditional uniform.

"Ah, Mr. Knight. Good to see the Marshals Service gave you adequate training."

Daniel gaped. "Priscilla, you're in on this?"

She leaned against the door and crossed her ankles, drawing attention to her sensible shoes. "You've no doubt learned this place is filled with one backstabber after another. Few can be trusted. The funny thing is, young ones always underestimate the old ones."

"You've been Anthony's trusted servant for years."

Priscilla nodded. "More than that. I've loved him all those years. I thought for sure he'd return my love. Especially after he learned of Evangelina's betrayal. Do you have any idea how many nights I comforted him as he wept wasted tears over her? I've never left his side. Never *asked* for anything. Never been *given* anything but empty promises. Even when he was behind prison bars." She sighed. "I took care of Giovanni, while Anthony longed for little Bella. She was a sweet baby. The only sunshine in this dark place. I, too, missed her and I owe you my gratitude for bringing her home. This is where she belongs."

Daniel watched Priscilla as she removed a combat knife from her apron pocket.

"Then help me get to her. Giovanni's going to kill her if I don't." He weighed the downturn of Priscilla's mouth. The wistful way she spoke about Anthony. Was she reminiscing? Or was she preparing to kill Daniel herself?

"You're correct. Giovanni will kill Bella. It's a good thing I was right about you. You love Bella."

"I'm just her handler," Daniel began, his heart drumming harder as the realization settled into his mind. He met her piercing blue eyes. "Yes, I do love Katie."

She smiled widely. "Yes, you do and that's why I'm here. Giovanni has taken her to their privately owned marina. He'll dump her body into the ocean and let nature take care of the evidence. Just as he did with his girlfriend."

"Giovanni said Anthony killed his girlfriend." Daniel gripped the gun, prepared to use it.

Priscilla slowly shook her head. Whose side was she on? "No, Giovanni grew tired of the commitment and realized she'd have access to his money—he doesn't share well—so he rid himself of her. Anyone who is a witness to his dealings is a liability." She held out her hand with the knife in her palm. "It's nothing like that thing." She gestured toward the MP5. "But good to have on hand anyway."

Daniel took the knife and slid it into his boot. "Do you have anything to tie up Lorenzo before he comes to?"

"Yes! I'll be right back." She scurried out the door and returned seconds later with a pair of handcuffs.

Questions battled for position in Daniel's brain but he pushed them aside. He slapped the cuffs around Lorenzo's wrists, then turned to face the maid.

Unfazed, she produced a small piece of paper. "I'm no Rand McNally, but here's a crude map to get you to the marina."

He glanced at the paper committing as much as possible to memory before shoving it into his pocket. "What about Lorenzo?" Daniel jerked his head toward the unconscious man.

"I'll lock the door. It won't hold him for long, but should buy you time. Go up the stairs and turn right. The door to the garage is at the end of the hall. Take the sedan. It's parked out front, keys are inside and the gate is open."

"Thank you."

"One last thing," Priscilla placed her hand on his shoulder. "When you get to Bella, confess your heart to her. I have a feeling she'll be receptive."

Daniel nodded.

"Now go!"

Hand pressed to his side, he bounded down the hallway, hoping Priscilla hadn't given him a death sentence. Her words lingered in his mind. He wouldn't let Katie go without telling her his growing feelings for her. Even if it meant leaving the Marshals. If she'd have him, he'd find another law enforcement career. The excitement and urgency blasted adrenaline through him.

Daniel readied the gun, cracking open the door. Only the warmth of the sun greeted him. Grateful, he ran toward the garage, target locked on the car. He noted the two missing vehicles—the pickup and the sports car. Using the buildings and other vehicles as cover, he bolted for the sedan and slid inside. In one fluid motion, he dropped the gun onto the passenger seat and started the engine.

Daniel slammed into Reverse and swung into a J-turn. The iron gate stood open as Priscilla had advised. He floored the pedal, speeding off the property.

He gripped the MP5 as he drew closer to the

familiar truck on the side of the road. Daniel reduced his speed and glanced around. Tires shredded, the vehicle appeared abandoned.

Had Katie escaped? He floored the pedal, glancing once more in his rearview mirror. No one followed. Was that too easy? Where were the other guards? No time for second-guessing.

Daniel accelerated, racing down the vacant road. Rescue scenarios bounced in his head as he searched for the private marina, praying he wasn't too late. Praying he had time to rescue the woman he loved.

SEVENTEEN

The duct tape cut into Katie's skin and the adhesive covering her mouth made breathing difficult. Anger kept her from succumbing to fear. She wanted to pummel Giovanni with her bound fists. If only he hadn't seat belted her in and taped her wrists to the door handle.

His loud music gave her a headache, adding to the blend of emotions twisting her stomach into knots. The gun was on his left side, and the two-seat sports car's interior was spotless except for the roll of duct tape at her feet.

Katie considered bumping the gearshift, but Giovanni drove at an excessive rate of speed. If she miscalculated and slid the transmission into Reverse, they'd end up rolling the car. The fiberglass body wouldn't hold up well on impact.

The rural land spanned endlessly. Too much open property, no other travelers and plenty of space to hide a body.

Her body.

Goose bumps covered her skin from the air conditioner blowing at full blast. The clock on the dashboard showed they'd been driving for thirty minutes. Thirty minutes away from Daniel. Her throat tightened at the last images of him in the garage. She had to get free. Had to get back to help Daniel.

Giovanni finally turned, stopping a football field's distance from the dark gray building surrounded by twenty-foot razor wire fence. He parked on the side of the road and turned down the music. "Don't want to get too close and attract the guards."

Katie scanned the area, and her gaze landed on the large identifying sign. This place was a prison. Hope abounded. Prisons had guards. Guards had guns. She scooted back in the seat and brought her feet up, slamming down on the dashboard. When that didn't prove effective, she reared back and kicked the windshield.

"Stop that!" Giovanni screeched, elbowing her in the nose.

The pain shocked Katie motionless, and she blinked hard against the stinging sensation.

Giovanni jerked her upright. "I thought you'd like to see where I got to spend most of my childhood." He motioned to the prison. "While other children played, went to the beach, and amusement parks, I sat inside that horrible place unable to even touch my father. All because of you."

Katie glared at him; her eyes watered from the throbbing in her nose.

"If you'd never been born, I wouldn't have had my childhood stolen. I wouldn't have been forced to know my father through a window!" Giovanni's hands shook as he tightly gripped the steering wheel. His expression darkened, and his square jaw flexed. The muscles in his neck were visible beneath the cotton shirt he wore.

Lord, help me. Katie closed her eyes. Think. Anthony and Priscilla were so wrong. Giovanni didn't want the locket. He wanted the impossible, time reversed.

The chime of Giovanni's cell phone interrupted his fit. He pulled the device from his pocket, swiped the screen and answered with a smile. "Excellent."

Katie leaned across the console, hoping to catch some of the conversation.

Giovanni gave her shoulder a hearty shove, pressing her against the door, and moved the phone to his left ear. "Stick to the plan." He disconnected and slid the phone into his pocket. "Time to go." He shifted into Drive and sped away from the prison.

His cryptic conversation left Katie with innumerable questions as her heart thrummed against her rib cage. She needed to get his phone. He'd have to let her out of the car at some point, and she'd be ready.

Giovanni sped along the coastline highway where the distant blue of the ocean framed their path.

He turned onto a dirt road and drove straight toward the water. Full leafy plants in all shades of green surrounded the vehicle. They bounced along the uneven road and Katie's teeth chattered from the jostling.

"I really must have this paved, although normally, I'd drive my truck. Thanks again for damaging it." Giovanni smacked the side of Katie's face with his palm.

She lurched away and shot him a menacing look, ignoring the burning on her cheek.

He laughed, parked the car and shut off the engine.

Katie swallowed hard, studying her surroundings. A twenty-foot black-and-white fishing boat was tied to the dock on the right. The long metal structure on the left appeared to hover over the waters like an enclosed tent. Was the place a giant garage for boats? Was there someone inside who would help her?

"Try to run, and I'll feed your body to the sharks," Giovanni warned as he pressed the power window button for her side. He threw open his door and stepped out.

Were there sharks here? She gazed out at the ocean.

The trunk opened and closed. Her stomach clenched as Giovanni leaned down outside her window. "I'm going to cut the tape. Do anything stupid, and I might slip and accidentally cut you." He displayed a knife that resembled a medieval war device. The gun wasn't in his hand and outrunning the knife was doable.

He reached inside, swiping the blade across the tape that held her to the door. Katie yanked her bound wrists free. Her pulse quickened as she prepared to bolt from the car.

"Good girl." Giovanni stepped back. "Get out."

Katie twisted in her seat, lifted the handle and kicked the door wide. The impact sent Giovanni sprawling flat on his back. She scrambled out of the car and ran toward the metal building.

Giovanni's footsteps pounded behind her.

She entered the structure and spotted a yellow speedboat. Her eyes darted about the interior searching for anything that would serve as a weapon.

He skidded around the corner, and bolted after her. "I'm going to kill you!"

She ran along the U-shaped wooden planks surrounding the boat.

"Little sister, you're starting to wear on my nerves." Giovanni stalked her, guarding the only way out of the building, opposite where she stood.

There was no place to run apart from the ocean, and her bound wrists restricted her ability to swim. She'd never be able to climb into the boat fast enough, and she didn't know how to start the engine anyway.

Giovanni lifted the gun and sent a blast at her feet.

She leaped to the side and glared at him.

"Next time, I won't pretend to miss. Walk slowly to me."

If he got her on the water, she'd have no hope of rescue. Take her chances in the ocean or return to Giovanni? She couldn't outrun a bullet or outswim a boat.

Death by bullet or drowning were the only available options, and both were terrifying. Katie grasped a corner of tape covering her mouth, ripped off the restrictive adhesive and inhaled deeply, filling her lungs. Then using her teeth, she tore at the unrelenting tape confining her wrists.

"You don't give up easily do you?" Giovanni taunted.

"If you're going to kill me, do it and get it over with. I'm done playing games with you." Katie continued to tug at the tape. A corner ripped free.

"Oh, I'm going to kill you unless you give me a reason not to."

Katie looked up. "What reason would that be?"

"Stop making me chase you, and I'll let your boyfriend go."

The ocean lapped at the speedboat.

"Prove it," Katie demanded.

Giovanni lifted his phone for her to see and made a call. At least it looked like he was making a call. "Change of plans. I'm feeling generous. Let Mr. Knight go. Yes, I'm serious." He tucked the phone into his jacket pocket.

Katie swallowed. Was he pretending? Had he called anyone?

"Proof enough?"

She glanced again at her options. If there was any chance at saving Daniel's life, she needed to try. Her life was as good as gone.

With resignation, she moved toward Giovanni.

His lips curved upward. "You're not as dumb as I thought." Grasping her arm, he shoved Katie in front of him, and tapped her head with the tip of the gun. "Just in case you think about running again, we're going to get the roll of duct tape out of the car. We'll need it for the trip."

"What about Daniel?" Katie walked to the car in reluctant obedience. The glimmer of the knife on the ground tempted her with another escape attempt.

"What about him?" Giovanni pushed by her and strode to the blade, kicking it away.

Katie frowned. He'd conned her. "You didn't call anyone, did you?"

"Nope."

She leaned inside the car and grabbed the tape.

"Go to the boat." Giovanni gestured toward the fishing boat held by ropes at the docks.

The current lapped at the shore with a sound that should have been soothing. Instead, the rhythmic swooshing reminded her that she'd be enveloped within its permanent grasp far too soon.

They made their way to the pier and the gently

rocking boat. A warm breeze blew through Katie's hair, and the ocean air engulfed her. Seagulls called from the sky, announcing her demise.

Would they set Daniel free? *Please, Lord, help us.* What if she bought time? Time for what? The authorities wouldn't find them before Giovanni rid himself of the sister he hated.

"Climb in and sit down." He leaned against the wooden pier, pointing to the boat with the Glock. "Hurry up!"

Katie got into the boat, sending death glares with her eyes.

"Sit there." He nodded to the bench seat at the back.

She moved toward the seat. Giovanni shoved her down and taped her wrists around the chrome railing.

Satisfied, he moved to the helm, started the engine and pulled away from the dock. "Ever been on the ocean before?"

She studied his joyful expression. He thought he'd won. Well, it wasn't over yet. *God, give me a way of escape.* She gripped the rail as the boat lurched into motion over the dark swirling ocean.

Giovanni increased speed, pelting water on her face as the giant skipping rock bounced over the waves.

Katie tightened her hold while he drove wildly, swerving from side to side without warning. She closed her eyes, fighting the queasiness.

The shore disappeared from sight and the ocean stretched beyond her imagination. A never-ending chasm of blue where no one would ever find her body. The reality hit hard as terror peaked with desperation and flatlined into sorrow.

Giovanni reduced the speed until they bobbed on the water. The engine quieted, and he faced Katie. His wide smile gave him a boyish appearance. His sports jacket and colored shirt were out of place and somehow, the man still looked like he'd stepped off the pages of a magazine. "There's nothing better than the ocean to relax me."

Sunlight bounced off the gun in his hand.

She couldn't swallow over the fear wedged in her throat.

Words vanished.

Logic was gone.

Fear ramped.

Giovanni narrowed his eyes and lifted the gun, targeting Katie. "Bang." He laughed. "Relax, little sister. I'm not going to kill you...yet."

Uncle Nick's training bounced to the forefront of her mind. *Agree with him. Do whatever he wants. Don't antagonize him.*

Giovanni walked to her and gazed past her. "I've dreamed of this moment. The ocean is beautiful, isn't it? Deep and enveloping. A wonderful grave, leaving bodies unrecoverable."

"Why are you doing this?" She shivered.

He shifted to the side and blinked at her. "I want you to suffer."

Katie's mind raced. "We're family, remember?"

His sardonic laugh echoed. "Family is the first to stab you in the back. Didn't our mother teach you that? She certainly taught it to me."

She forced calmness into her words. "But I've never done anything to you. I didn't even know you existed. You could've gone on with your life, free of me. You still can."

"True, except Father wouldn't let it go." Giovanni stood, swaying with the ocean's movement.

"I don't want the business or the money. I'm sorry for what Mama did to you. No child deserves to be abandoned." Katie tilted her head and managed a sympathetic tone. "You said yourself she was mentally ill. I'm sorry she hurt you."

"Are you?" Giovanni moved to her side. His expression softened.

Hope returned. She'd negotiate her way out of this.

He knelt in front of her and hissed, "I'm sorry *you* were ever born."

Katie gaped and fear turned to indignation. Submission wouldn't help her. Giovanni was the epitome of evil.

He got to his feet and leaned against the side of the boat.

She lifted her chin. "You might recall that I wasn't the one who came looking for me. I was perfectly happy not knowing about any of this. I've lived twenty-four years oblivious to you or Anthony. There's nothing that I want, so you can let Daniel and I go, and take the entire estate for yourself."

"No, I can't. As long as you're alive, you have the deciding share of Marino Industries."

"I'll give it back to you."

Giovanni's jaw tightened, and he stepped forward, his dark eyes blazing. "Am I your charity case? Understand this, Isabella, you'll never take anything away from me again."

Katie's words tumbled out rapid-fire. "I'll give you the locket, then you'll be rich."

"I'm already rich, little sister. That locket is nothing more than a fairy-tale Father believes. I've made a real fortune by myself, and let's face it, money rules the world."

This man was insane, and she was dead. Katie shivered, arms aching from the restraints and position. She forced the words from her mouth. "Giovanni, I care about you and I want to be a family."

He ripped the tape from her wrists and pressed the gun against her forehead. "You're the reason Mother left me an orphaned little boy!" he cried.

He was an overgrown child having a psychotic tantrum.

Katie blinked. Her brother was delusional. Crazy. You can't negotiate with crazy, but she had to try. "You're a brilliant businessman. You're the reason Marino Industries is so profitable. Anthony relies on you. Show him that he's made the wrong choice by giving me the deciding shares. I don't have a clue about business. He'll be so disgusted with me and gladly revert control to you. I know you'll impress him. Besides, if you kill me, what will happen when Anthony discovers what you've done?"

Giovanni stepped back, gun still trained on her, and inhaled deeply, regaining composure. "Good try. I may have underestimated your negotiation skills. However, I've already thought of that. Father will think his poor, sweet Bella ran away. Didn't he offer you a chance to escape?"

Sweat dripped into Katie's eyes.

"What? You thought he would hide something from his only son?"

Priscilla's words about greed being an insatiable taskmaster rose in her mind. "Did Anthony tell you about the money hidden away?"

Giovanni's grin faded.

"There are numbers inside the locket. Account numbers where Mama stashed millions."

"You're a liar."

"What reason would I have to lie about that, especially now? It's all true. Take me back to the house, and I'll show you where it is." Katie spotted an air tank inches from where she sat. She held her breath.

Giovanni raised an eyebrow. "Where's the locket? I'll have my men find it."

"Take me to the house."

"Little sister, you're wearing on my patience."

Katie feigned surrender. "Fine, take the tape off and I'll show you."

"You have it with you?"

She nodded.

Giovanni walked to her and with one hand, ripped off the tape.

Katie delivered a solid kick to his stomach, causing him to stumble against the driver's seat. She jumped up and grasped the air tank, slamming it down on his head.

Giovanni slumped to the floor of the boat, releasing his hold on the gun.

Katie snagged the weapon, aimed at him and moved to the boat controls. Which was the right one to make the boat go?

Hesitation cost Katie the precious moment Giovanni needed. He grabbed her from behind, jerked her away from the wheel and tossed Katie overboard.

Daniel sped the sedan down the dirt road toward the ocean in front of him. Would he ever get there? He'd been driving for what seemed like hours. The dusty air and purr of the engine would announce his presence so there wouldn't be any tiptoeing to rescue Katie. He'd rely on God and the MP5 to take care of any hostile welcoming committee.

Though no one had followed thus far, they would be. Priscilla couldn't hold Marino's minions off for long. He'd face their wrath when they discovered Lorenzo.

In the long drive, he hadn't passed a gas station or any sign of civilization. He needed to call for backup but there was no time to go off on his own volition. Time was running out.

He'd finally found the woman of his dreams, and he would fight for her. He couldn't…wouldn't lose Katie.

The marina had to be close. He glanced down at Priscilla's crude map. Had she sent him on an aimless mission? No. She'd said it was a remote location.

The car bounced over the rocky terrain, slamming into the occasional pothole. Each jostle inflamed his injured ribs. Daniel did his best to ignore the pain.

He skidded around the turn where the road opened to a wide parking area. The gleaming sports car sat near the docks, like a blaring siren announcing Giovanni's presence. The only other object was a large metal boat shed but the entrance was out of his line of sight. The sedan, though quiet, was far from stealth so if there was anyone inside, they'd have heard him coming.

Daniel parked and killed the engine. The knife

Priscilla had given him was inside his boot and he clutched the gun. Only the sound of crashing waves filled the air.

He slid out of the car and crept toward the sports car. The keys still hung in the ignition.

Daniel scanned the marina, focusing on the boat shed. Gun poised, he made his way inside and paused at the sight of a yellow speedboat bobbing between the U-shaped wooden deck.

He cleared the area, and confirmed it was empty except for an out-of-place piece of duct tape stuck to the floor. Daniel inspected the adhesive. Had Katie been here? Where was she now?

Daniel raced back out of the shelter and spotted ropes swaying from the pier. A second boat? If Priscilla was right, Giovanni didn't plan on returning with Katie. But what about the boat? Would someone else pick him up in the speedboat?

His gaze landed on the sedan. He ran to the car, started the engine and drove through the brush. With the vehicle hidden behind the boat shed, he sprinted back inside. Snatching several tarps from the shelf against the wall, Daniel rushed out and spread the plastic to disguise the car. He finished by placing branches he'd ripped from the trees on top of the tarps.

Last, he returned to the sports car and pulled the keys from the ignition and tossed them into the water. No sense in giving Giovanni easy access to a getaway vehicle.

A cloud of dust and a vehicle in the distance caught his attention. The classic foreign car approached at a high rate of speed. He glanced again at the shed and scurried around the wall. The car's tires on the gravel and the purring engine grew louder.

Daniel's adrenaline flowed like lava.

He pressed against the hot steel of the boat shed, gun ready. His mind raced with response options and attack plans. If he took out whoever was coming, he wouldn't know where to find Giovanni and Katie. Couldn't give the criminal a chance to escape. Timing was crucial. Changing course, he rushed to the shelves, snagged another tarp, and climbed inside the speedboat.

Daniel covered himself with the tarp and waited.

One door slammed.

A man's voice sang—out of tune.

A single adversary turned the odds in Daniel's favor.

The man boarded the boat and shuffled around before starting the engine.

Daniel peeked out from the tarp's cover, watching The Professor behind the helm.

Patience.

Finally, the engine hummed to life, and they exited the boat shed.

A few more seconds.

The Professor drove with ease across the massive waves, increasing his speed. When the engine noise roared at full blast, Daniel pushed the tarp aside and crept toward the oblivious man.

Daniel's arm shot out like a tentacle, wrapping around The Professor's throat, and rested the MP5's muzzle against his head. "Where's your gun?"

The Professor's voice was calm. "Hello, Mr. Knight. It's in my hip holster."

Daniel yanked the gun out and tossed it into the water.

"Well played."

"Where's Katie?" Daniel tightened his choke hold.

"She's with Giovanni and he's expecting me. Then he'll toss her body out to the fishies." The Professor chuckled.

"I guess we'd better not waste any time." He pressed the gun tighter against the man's head. "Why is he waiting for you? Why not drive back to shore after he tosses Katie overboard?"

"That's not the plan. He'll need a ride back to shore."

Confirmation of Daniel's assumption. "He's planning on leaving Katie out in the middle of the ocean in a boat?" What was he missing?

"Something like that. I give you kudos for your bravery. Although, I'd call it foolhardiness," The Professor called over the loud engine.

The boat slammed down on a wave.

Daniel gritted his teeth against the pain pulsating from his ribs. He shifted his arm to keep pressure against the wounded side. "Funny, I'd say working for a criminal is stupid."

"What do you think will happen when Giovanni sees you? He won't hand Isabella over without a fight."

Daniel considered the words. He needed a bargaining chip. Had Katie already told Giovanni she had the locket?

"I'm sure you've thought of something." The Professor gripped the wheel.

The MP5 was a great convincer and Giovanni wasn't expecting him. If The Professor alerted him to Daniel's presence, he'd lose the element of surprise.

He gripped the gun, slamming the butt against The Professor's head. The man slumped to the floor of the boat. Daniel grasped the steering wheel. In a perfect world, he'd toss The Professor overboard, but his injured rib prohibited that option. He hoped The Professor stayed unconscious. Another glance at the man had him debating slowing the boat to secure restraints. No time. Daniel would have to take his chances because nothing would stop him from getting to Katie.

EIGHTEEN

Katie inhaled a mouthful of water before she had the chance to hold her breath. She swam for the surface, bursting through like a dolphin, and spit out the salty liquid. The waves thrust around her and she treaded in a fury to stay above them.

The boat's engine roared to life, and Giovanni spun in the opposite direction.

Her heart drummed in a panicked tempo.

He was leaving!

Alarm morphed into confusion as he changed course. Giovanni was coming back. Too fast. Dashing right toward her.

Katie dove and swam lower avoiding the vicious swirling blades. She waited in the engulfing blue until her lungs burned from lack of oxygen.

Unable to hold her breath another second, she kicked upward, away from the boat. Once she broke through, Katie sucked in air and oriented herself. Like a shark circling its prey, Giovanni drove around her forcing the water into motion.

After several rounds, he reduced the speed, bobbing out of reach. "I was almost duped into believing you about the locket." His form was silhouetted against the sky.

"What if I'm not lying? Are you willing to risk losing millions of dollars?"

The engine hummed as he drew closer, and

she could see him clearly. Blood streamed down the side of his head where she'd hit him. Crimson marred his perfect features and accented his reptilian smile. "There is no necklace."

"Yes, there is. I have it in my pocket but I can't grab it while treading water. You'll have to let me back into the boat."

Silent minutes passed before he approached. Katie wanted to be stubborn and refuse the offered respite, but sheer exhaustion forced her to cooperate.

Inches from grasping the edge of the boat, Giovanni shifted into Reverse and roared with laughter. "I'm not nearly as gullible as you. No wonder Mother and her lover found it so easy to lie to you. Give up. You're going to die and I'm going to love watching it happen."

She closed her eyes. What reason did she have to live, anyway? She was alone and Giovanni would kill Daniel. There was nothing left for her. Daniel's words from the day on the Manitou Incline touched Katie like a life raft, reminding her she could do anything since completing the climb. "Lord, give me strength. Rescue me."

"Glad Mother paid for swimming lessons," Giovanni's heckling words echoed.

A breeze whispered over her as the warm water filtered through her fingers. Giovanni's taunts faded into the background, becoming white noise.

Greed is a selfish, insatiable taskmaster. Katie

took a deep breath. "Too bad Anthony kept the locket's secret from you. He must've planned to keep the money for himself."

Giovanni's pause said she'd hit her mark. "If you're lying, I promise your death won't be quick. Neither will Mr. Knight's."

Katie eyed the gun. "Daniel is alive though?"

"For now," Giovanni smirked.

Squeezing her eyes shut, sorrow swooped and clung to Katie's shoulders. She'd never get to tell Daniel how she felt. Yet the climb in Colorado, their walk along the beach and every moment in between had awakened her heart to the beauty of falling in love. For that, she was eternally grateful to Daniel.

Giovanni moved toward her again, helping her into the boat. Shivering, she dropped onto the passenger seat.

"Let me see the locket."

Katie dug out the necklace from her pocket. An idea sprang to mind. As Giovanni reached to snatch it from her hand, she tossed the locket to the floor. It slid along the moist fiberglass to the opposite end of the boat.

Giovanni roared, driving his fist into her nose. Stunned, Katie fell backward.

He turned to retrieve the necklace. She lunged, landing on his back. With her arms wrapped around his neck, she drove her fingers into his eyes. Giovanni screamed, tearing at her arms.

He lost hold of the locket and it plunged into the ocean depths.

Giovanni yanked Katie over his shoulder and body-slammed her to the floor.

The last thing she saw was his fist before everything went black.

Daniel sped toward the black-and-white bobbing vessel, slowing as he recognized Giovanni and Katie. He gripped the MP5.

Katie sat strapped to the helm, head drooping. Unconscious? Fury propelled him. *Please be alive.*

Giovanni stood next to her, gun aimed at Daniel, holding a red duffel bag. "Mr. Knight, don't do anything rash. This bomb could go off any second."

Katie groaned and looked up, blood streamed from her nose.

Grateful she was alive and infuriated at her injuries, Daniel wanted to take her into his arms and never let go. The realization burst through him like Fourth of July fireworks. He *loved* Katie Tribani.

"Daniel!" Katie cried. "You're alive! Oh, thank God!"

Giovanni set the duffel onto her lap. "What a delight you could join us."

"Spare me." Daniel glowered.

Behind him, The Professor groaned.

"Get up," Daniel ordered. The man rocked slightly with the waves. "Stand in front of me."

The Professor obeyed.

Giovanni's eyes narrowed. "Are all my men incompetent? No matter. I've built in contingencies. Show him your phone, Isaac."

"Isaac?" Daniel murmured. "I prefer The Professor."

"Clever," Isaac grumbled.

"Don't move." Daniel jabbed the man's head with the gun.

"You'll want to see what I have," Isaac argued.

If Giovanni moved an inch one way or the other, he'd have a clear shot. The danger of setting off the bomb kept Daniel from pulling the trigger.

"Show him his sister." Giovanni pressed the gun barrel against Katie's temple. "Or do you need more motivation?"

Daniel frowned. "Move cautiously."

Isaac pulled a cell phone from his sports coat pocket with exaggerated sluggishness, swiped the screen and held up the device.

Brittany sat propped against a cement wall—a way too familiar setting—dressed in skimpy clothes, a skeleton of a human. Her long blond hair hung limply, and makeup smeared her pale face. Fury burned through Daniel. He reached for the phone.

Giovanni sent a shot, whizzing inches from him. "Now, now, that's not yours."

Isaac chuckled, tucking the device into his pocket. "Told you so."

"What is it?" Katie's voice was shaky.

Daniel clenched his teeth. "Where is she?" He knew the answer. Knew he'd been so close to rescuing her. Why hadn't Priscilla told him?

"I've always heard that siblings have a natural connection. I'm surprised you didn't sense Brittany's presence, in the very next room where you were held."

"You're a liar. That picture could've been taken anywhere. Or you could've moved her." The words weren't convincing in Daniel's ears. For once, he knew Giovanni spoke the truth.

"Are you sure? Tell you what, let's make a trade. Your life for your sister's."

"I'm not making any deals with you. Give me Katie before I shoot you and finish this twisted game." Daniel shook with rage.

"You and Isabella will share a fate. However, I'm not completely without compassion. Your sister's worth nothing to me. The bigger question is whether she's worth something to you?" Giovanni waved Isaac over. "Secure Mr. Knight."

Isaac shifted and Daniel leveled the gun between the criminals. "Take one more step and I'll test the trigger."

Giovanni sighed. "You're wasting valuable time."

"You'll kill Brittany because she can expose you." Daniel's mind raced with options.

"She's so inebriated, she doesn't have a clue where she is. I can drop her off on the same corner I picked her up and she'll be fine," Giovanni answered.

Daniel's neck warmed at the insinuation.

Katie's eyes pleaded with him. "Daniel, save your sister."

"Listen to her." Giovanni cooed. "I'm a businessman, remember? I'm giving you a surefire deal. And please hurry. The bomb's on a timed detonation device, set to blow in about…eight minutes. We can continue this ridiculous standoff and all of us will die. Or, Mr. Knight, you can trade places with me and save poor Brittany."

Katie nodded.

"Tick tock," Giovanni taunted.

"Daniel, it's the right thing to do," Katie implored.

"I'll agree if you let Katie go too," Daniel said.

Giovanni shook his head. "Nope, that's not going to happen. Hand Isaac your gun now. One. Two."

Impossible choices, but he had to do something. Daniel shoved the MP5 at Isaac.

He grinned, jabbing the gun between Daniel's shoulder blades. "Let's shoot them and save ourselves a boat."

"Your opinion is neither appreciated nor required," Giovanni said. "Transfer Mr. Knight over here."

Isaac frowned and complied, jerking Daniel's arm upward.

Daniel cried out at the blaze that radiated from his ribs. Isaac took the opportunity to drive a punch into the already inflamed area. Taking flex-cuffs from under a hidden seat compartment, he tied Daniel's wrists together.

"Move."

Daniel slid awkwardly across to the fishing boat with Isaac following. When they reached the back, Giovanni tossed Isaac a rope, and he bound Daniel to the railing.

"Good job," Giovanni praised.

Isaac gave Daniel a toothy grin at the compliment as Giovanni climbed into the speedboat.

How many minutes had passed?

"Enjoy your last moments." Isaac laughed, turning to join his boss.

Giovanni pointed the gun at Isaac and his grin fell. "You're going to keep Mr. Knight and my sister company."

"But I—" Isaac paled.

"I won't tolerate incompetence." Giovanni pulled the trigger, silencing Isaac.

The man tumbled into Daniel's legs and rolled to the floor.

Giovanni shifted the speedboat into gear and jetted away.

"Mr. Knight," Isaac gasped.

Katie's eyes widened. "He's still alive."

"I guess I didn't choose the winning side either." He attempted a laugh only to suffer a bout of coughing. Red seeped through his fingers.

"How do we disarm the bomb?" Daniel bent his leg to the side, removing the knife from his boot. He twisted and slid the knife behind him, sawing at the flex-cuffs.

Isaac grimaced. "Brittany is at the house."

"The bomb!" Daniel pressed. His angst worked against his fine motor skills, and he dropped the knife. Bending, he grasped hold and returned to cutting through the plastic.

Isaac shook his head. "It's on a timer. You can't. Shut it off."

"Untie us!" Katie screeched.

"I'm sorry, Isabella." Isaac dragged himself toward her, tugging at her restraints.

"Please. Hurry!"

The knife slipped through, releasing Daniel from the plastic restraints. He jumped up and rushed to Katie.

"Is Isaac…?" She blinked.

Daniel glanced down. Isaac's lifeless eyes stared past him. "Yes."

He grabbed the duffel bag's handle, flung it away from the boat, then sliced through Katie's restraints. She moved from the steering wheel allowing Daniel to shift into Drive. They sped toward the shore as an explosion rocked the waters.

* * *

Katie turned to see the mushroom of water burst into the air.

They slammed against the rough waves. Daniel pressed his arm against his left side. Each hit on the water appeared to make him flinch.

"Here, let me drive." She took over the wheel, surprised he didn't argue.

"Katie, I need to tell you something."

"Okay?" She focused on steering the boat.

"I love you. And when this is all over, and I'm holding you in my arms, I'm going to show you just how much."

Warmth radiated through Katie. "I love you too." She clung to the boat to keep from lunging into his arms. "But...what about your career?"

"Let's get Brittany, then I'll fill you in on my idea."

She shook her head and bit her lip, silently disagreeing. "I can't believe you got away."

Daniel glanced at her. "I owe that to Priscilla. She knew all about Giovanni's plan. Turns out Lorenzo's quite the entrepreneur willing to work for the highest bidder. We had a little heart-to-heart."

She quirked an eyebrow. "Looks more like a fist-to-face."

Daniel chuckled. "That bad?"

"Uh, yeah."

"Let's hope Isaac's cell phone still works." He knelt and removed the device from the dead man's pocket.

Katie shivered, whispering a prayer.

"Battery's almost dead." Daniel hollered over the engine noise into the phone. "Chief, it's Daniel. We're headed to Marino's Florida mansion." He paused. "It's a long story."

Another pause.

"Negative, sir. Giovanni will kill Brittany."

Katie hit a wave and Daniel clutched his side.

"Sorry," she whispered.

"Please, Chief, send help." Daniel studied the screen. "Pray he heard that before the phone died. It's against my better judgment, but I can't risk losing Brittany."

"We're a great team. If nothing else, we'll buy time until help arrives." Katie pointed to the yellow speedboat, parked at the docks.

"Go slow. Be ready to speed out of here if I say so." Daniel searched for any movement. "Looks deserted and the foreign car's missing. Giovanni's gone. Go ahead and dock."

"How do you know he isn't waiting for us? His sports car's still there." She pulled alongside the wooden dock.

"Because I tossed his keys into the ocean. He had to take the foreign car Isaac drove." Daniel grabbed the MP5 and checked the magazine. He jumped out, securing the boat to the dock.

Together, they ran to the hidden sedan.

"Good job with camouflage," Katie said.

Once the coverings were removed, they climbed into the car with Daniel driving. He raced out of the marina. "Giovanni's arrogant enough to believe his plan is fail-proof. I'll drop you off at the nearest public place. Call for help while I go to the Marino house and rescue Brittany."

Katie shot him a look. "We're finishing this together. Besides, whether you're willing to admit it or not, you're hurt and need my help."

The corner of Daniel's lip curved, and the dimple returned to his cheek.

A flutter in Katie's stomach reminded her to refocus while awakening her to the truth. She'd fallen for Daniel Knight. The thought gave her pause. She was head-over-common-sense-crazy for him.

"No sign of dust ahead means Giovanni has a good head start," Daniel advised.

"I realized something when Giovanni didn't believe me about the locket. He had no idea it had any worth. That means he wasn't the one who sent the attacker into my room last night."

Daniel met her eyes. "Anthony ordered the attack."

She nodded and swallowed. "Giovanni's a psychotic maniac and I haven't liked him from the beginning, but Anthony's worse. I almost believed he was protecting me and wanted us to be a family. He was only using me to get to the locket."

NINETEEN

Daniel floored the pedal; he couldn't get to the Marino home fast enough. He parked a half mile outside the property under a grove of trees. "I'll walk from here. The sedan's quiet but I'm not taking chances of them spotting us before we're ready."

"Agreed except *we'll* walk in there." Katie jaw was taut. "And *we* can't go blasting in there with only one gun."

Daniel frowned. "Exactly, that's why *you're* going to stay here. Backup should arrive soon."

"No." Katie reached for the door handle.

She was beautiful and ornery. He'd tell her so... later. "How am I supposed to protect you if you keep disagreeing with me?"

"We're a team and who knows? Maybe I'm supposed to protect *you*." Katie grinned.

Daniel groaned. "Stay with me and do what I say without argument. Got it?"

"Yes, sir." She saluted.

They exited the car and kept close to the abundance of foliage around the estate, moving along the iron fence.

"What do we do if the gate's closed?"

Daniel didn't want to think of the possibilities. There was no way he could climb the fence in his condition. "Pray it's open."

A large bush at the front of the entrance gave them a place to hide. The heat bore down on them, and salty perspiration burned the lacerations on Daniel's face.

"It didn't seem this far away in the car."

Daniel grinned. "C'mon, flatlander. This is no Manitou Incline. Keep up."

She winked and his pulse increased.

He peered through the iron rods, spotting the foreign car parked in front of the house. The gate stood open and there were no guards.

Daniel placed a hand on Katie's shoulder, halting her. "We don't know if anyone's watching the cameras. I'm counting on Giovanni's assumption that the explosion killed us. Otherwise, he'd have waited to finish us off."

Katie nodded. "Right."

"Stay flat against the house and behind the plants as much as possible."

Large-leafed vegetation lined the familiar gray patio where they'd first been introduced to the Marinos. Slate steps snaked their way up the side of the house.

Katie and Daniel ducked behind the various decorative shrubberies, cautiously making their way up the steps. At the top, they moved toward the patio, using the home's white stucco walls to hide them. Daniel put a finger to his lips. Katie nodded.

He peered around the corner of the house. Lorenzo stood with his back to the glass doors in his familiar holding-a-gun-against-his-chest pose. Guess it was too much to hope he was still unconscious and handcuffed in the cement room.

The sun glaring off the windows made it impossible to see inside from Daniel's vantage point. He inched around the wall, pausing when he ran out of stucco.

"Giovanni, please don't do this," Priscilla's voice pleaded.

"You're a stupid woman. Always in the way. Never knowing your place," Giovanni berated.

"Son," Anthony's voice.

"Don't call me son! I have been loyal to you. Faithfully by your side, and you show your love for me by favoring Isabella?"

"She is my daughter," Anthony argued.

"I am your son!" Giovanni screeched.

He was emotional. Losing control. Excellent.

"She is all I have left of Evangelina. My one true love." Anthony's words were barely audible.

"Anthony, no," Priscilla urged.

"And what was I?" Giovanni asked.

"You are my son and I love you. Your mother loves you," Anthony calmly responded.

"My mother is dead!" Giovanni bawled.

Daniel held his place, listening for the moment he'd exploit and attack. Was Brittany inside the room with them? He hadn't heard her voice. Giovanni no doubt kept her drugged, so she was probably unconscious somewhere. Unconscious he could live with… *Please don't let her be dead.*

"Priscilla is your mother," Anthony interjected.

Daniel jerked his head toward Katie, meeting her baffled expression. Had he heard Anthony correctly?

"What. Did. You. Say?" Giovanni's low tone carried tremulous rage.

"We agreed we'd never tell you or Isabella. Evangelina cared for you like you were her own." Anthony's voice trembled.

"My mother is the maid?" Giovanni roared.

Daniel scooted closer to the doorway. He was stopped by two loud pops from inside.

Katie scurried behind him.

He swallowed.

"No!" Anthony wailed. "Priscilla! Giovanni… why?"

"I will not be reduced to the son of a pathetic servant." Wrath hung in Giovanni's steady voice.

"Why would I lie?" Anthony's cries were choked with an emotion Daniel couldn't quite name.

"You lie to everyone. Your precious Isabella believed your ramblings about that ridiculous necklace. She almost had me convinced." Giovanni's wicked laugh boomed through the open glass doors. "She said your *maid* told her the locket held the key to stolen money. As if I'd believe that! Oh, well, it's gone now."

"I knew it! Priscilla didn't believe me, but I knew Bella had it," Anthony pressed. "Wait, what do you mean it's gone?"

Daniel shot a sideways glance at Katie, the sadness evident in her eyes.

"I dropped it into the ocean when she attacked me."

"You lost a priceless heirloom?" Anthony's voice rose an octave. "Do you have any idea what you've done?" His deep grief-stricken wails reached them.

"Stop crying like a little girl. What's done is done," Giovanni scolded.

"Millions. You lost millions," Anthony moaned.

"It was true?" Giovanni's question was less confident.

Anthony's howls rose. "Yes, it was true!"

"One more secret you kept from me?"

Daniel caught a glimpse of Katie out of the corner of his eye. Her jaw was tight and her eyes narrow.

Anthony spoke desperate words. "I was going to surprise you. We'd start over. Go to Australia or Brazil."

"Liar! You planned to take the money and leave me. Again! If you'd been honest I might've reconsidered killing you." Giovanni's threat hung in the humid air.

Daniel leaned closer to get a view of the room,

but he couldn't see anything without compromising his position. He held up his hand to still Katie.

"I've given you everything you ever wanted," Anthony argued.

"Your devotion was never to me. No matter how good I was or what I accomplished. You only cared about Isabella." Giovanni's ranting continued, "How's it feel to know your precious daughter had the locket and kept it from you? Like father like daughter."

Daniel inched around, moved from the cover of the house and slid behind tall foliage outside the glass doors. With steady movements, he peered around the plant's dinner-plate-size leaves.

"My son, we're great together. Think this through. You're right, with Isabella out of the picture, you'd be my sole heir," Anthony negotiated. "Even now you have immense control over the business. Stop this craziness and let's build our fortune without interfering women."

Lorenzo's back to Daniel gave him limited advantage. Anthony sat tied to a chair, also with his back to the window. Priscilla was sprawled on the floor by Anthony's feet. Blood pooled beneath her. Where was Brittany? Still in the cement cell? Where was Zach? Or the tobacco-smelling guard? He needed clear passage into the house.

Giovanni paced with a gun in his grip.

Daniel calculated his next move; it had to be

precise to avoid a shootout that could result in hurting Katie or Giovanni escaping.

"Sorry, Father, I don't need you anymore. Without you and Isabella, I'm free to enjoy the entire inheritance. Why would I want to give that up?" Giovanni leered.

Anthony shook his head. "Except for the clause I added."

"What clause?" Giovanni spoke through clenched teeth.

"The clause that says if anything should happen to Isabella or me—outside of natural causes—you get nothing."

Giovanni's murderous glare zeroed in on Anthony. He stood frozen in place. The news clearly threw him off. "That can't be. I checked with Edward this morning before he left."

"I made the adjustment over the phone as soon as you dragged Isabella from the house. Do you think your ideas are new? That your covetous ways aren't written in the way you act?" Anthony baited Giovanni.

Daniel aimed the gun at Lorenzo and mouthed "stay here" to Katie.

She nodded.

"You ruin everything!" Giovanni's face contorted, and he lunged at his father. The gun dropped to the ground as he plummeted the elderly man with both fists.

The out-of-control moment was exactly what Daniel needed.

Sirens in the distance acted like a pause button. Giovanni stopped in the middle of his bout and ran from the room, likely looking out the front door.

Daniel rushed Lorenzo from behind, tackling him to the ground. His weapon skidded across the marble floor. Refusing to surrender to the pain in his side, Daniel got to his feet and aimed the MP5 at Lorenzo.

Lorenzo scrambled on the ground, groping for the gun that lay out of his reach. Katie lunged, securing it and faced Daniel.

"Nice," Daniel praised.

Katie kept the gun trained on Lorenzo and for the briefest moment, Daniel wondered if she knew how to shoot.

Anthony's head hung with his chin to his chest.

Giovanni ran back into the room. "Lorenzo, we have to—"

"Hello, brother," Katie said.

"You're both dead...the bomb," Giovanni mumbled.

"Wrong." Daniel smirked, enjoying the moment.

Two police officers rushed into the house. "Drop the weapons!"

Katie and Daniel lowered their guns to the floor, lifting their hands above their heads.

"These people are intruders. They attacked my bodyguard," Giovanni accused as an officer shoved him against the wall, handcuffing him.

"I'm US Marshal Daniel Knight. This is Katie Tribani." Daniel stood, arms still raised.

A tall, slender officer entered and strode to Daniel. "Marshal Knight, Chief Bridges called in. I'm Sergeant Wes Crayton." He waved off the officers. "They're good."

"Giovanni would've killed your sister if I hadn't intervened," Lorenzo interjected.

Daniel spun to face him. "Are you seriously playing the hero?"

"I helped your sister and I could've killed you but didn't. I spared your life. Giovanni wanted you dead from the beginning. Isabella too. Put in a good word for me. You owe me," Lorenzo whined.

Daniel snorted. "I don't owe you anything. You're pathetic."

Lorenzo sneered as an officer grabbed him and slapped cuffs on his wrists, dragging him from the room.

"Please check on Priscilla," Daniel called over his shoulder. "I've got to get my sister."

Sergeant Crayton and Daniel raced through the house, down the stairs and into the hallway. He tugged at the locked door.

"Step back." Crayton aimed his gun and fired.

The door swung open, and Daniel rushed in sliding to his knees at Brittany's side. Zach lay unconscious in the corner. "He's another of Marino's guards, but there's one missing."

Daniel cradled Brittany's fragile body and shallow breaths confirmed she was alive. "Thank God. Please stay with me, Brit," he whispered, lifting and carrying her up the stairs.

"Paramedics are outside," Crayton informed, cuffing Zach as another officer dragged him from the room.

Daniel rushed to a female EMT standing beside an ambulance, and placed Brittany inside. "I don't know what they drugged her with."

The EMT nodded. "We'll take good care of her."

He nodded appreciation, not trusting himself to speak.

Another paramedic pushed Anthony out of the house on a stretcher. "Thank you, Daniel Knight." He held out his hand.

Daniel refused the gesture. "I didn't do it for you." He stormed past.

Katie met him at the door. "Priscilla's still alive!"

He exhaled gratitude.

A paramedic called out orders and pushed past them, wheeling Priscilla out on a stretcher.

Daniel held Katie close as they watched the ambulance speed off the property, its screeching sirens blaring the urgency of Priscilla's condition.

"They'll take good care of her," Crayton assured.

"I hope so. I owe her my life." Daniel swallowed the lump in his throat, praying for the brave woman who lived a life of secrets to save the ones she loved.

A light breeze blew over Katie's shoulders. She rubbed her arms to ward off the chill. Standing on the hospital's patio, she gazed out over the city as the sun began its descent. The events of the past few days flipped through her mind, reminding Katie that she hadn't finished grieving.

Thoughts of Mama and the cost she'd paid to be free of the Marinos rushed at Katie. Tears welled in her eyes. The anger she'd held was gone, replaced by a deep admiration for her mother's bravery. Katie welcomed the release. The truth had truly set her free.

Heavy footsteps drew closer.

She turned and cringed.

Daniel's gait was sluggish and a butterfly bandage covered the cut on his eye. A compression wrap encircled his torso.

"That's a fashionable look."

"For your information, this is the latest in Paris. It's the fall line for torn cartilage and cracked ribs." He laughed and winced, holding his side. "Don't make me laugh. It hurts too much."

She grinned, helping him to sit in the metal patio chair. "Shouldn't you be resting?"

Daniel shifted in the seat, obviously hurting.

"I'll rest when I get home. Pain's a good reminder that I'm alive."

"I'm not sure the doctor would agree."

"Probably not but after all the probing, tests and X-rays, he's cleared me to leave. Just waiting on Brittany's release, then we'll head to the airport."

"Did they give you pain meds?"

He grimaced. "Yes, but I haven't taken them. Didn't want to dull my senses."

"Don't make me request an injection for you."

Daniel held up his hands in surrender and groaned. "I'll take the meds. I promise. No needles please."

She laughed, pulling over a chair to join him.

"How're you doing?"

Katie redirected his question. "Have you heard from Sergeant Crayton?"

"Anthony's stable although he's still moaning about Giovanni losing the locket."

"Wow, talk about obsessive. Has he even asked about Giovanni or Priscilla?"

"According to the guards outside his door, he keeps crying about his losses. To be fair, he's lost everything, or he will by the time this is over. Edward's willing to testify to save himself. Sergeant Crayton said the Marinos' bodyguards have all been apprehended and singing to save themselves."

"Anthony and Giovanni live in a world plagued

with lies and half-truths. I wonder if anyone in their group knows what truth is."

Daniel snorted. "No doubt about that."

"Hard to imagine losing that kind of wealth. I can't even fathom what I'd have done with the billions from the locket."

"Really? No ideas?"

Katie tilted her head. "Well, I did have an idea to help women and children who spend considerable time in witness protection. I'd like to create a program that educates them in acclimating to the outside world. If Mama had a way to tell me the truth, maybe she would have. Fear kept her imprisoned and left me oblivious."

"That's a great idea. I think you should make it happen."

Katie sighed. "Too bad the locket's buried under the ocean."

"Never underestimate the possibilities." Daniel shifted again.

"So, what'll happen to Anthony and Giovanni?"

"They're being charged with kidnapping and attempted murder to start. I'm sure there will be more charges to follow. They won't see freedom again soon, if ever."

"And Priscilla?"

"She's out of surgery still in critical condition."

Sadness and relief passed over Katie. "Will she be charged with anything?"

"Depends on how much she actually knew, but

if she's willing to testify against the Marinos it might help her."

"I can't imagine her going against either Anthony or Giovanni, even to save herself jail time. Do you think she will?"

"I don't know—her devotion runs deep." Daniel met her eyes. "Now, quit ignoring my question. How're you doing?"

Katie pushed up from the chair, pacing between Daniel and the patio's iron railing. She wrapped herself in a hug. "My brain's on overload."

"I'm sure."

"I never thanked you for rescuing me."

"Well, me and God."

She loved the way he spoke openly about his faith. "He's amazing that way."

"I talked with Chief Bridges. The leak has been identified. You'll have to return to witness protection until it's determined you're no longer in danger."

Katie considered his words. "It's not like I have any place else to go." She bit her lip. Speaking her fears made them real. Not knowing was worse.

"What's wrong?" Daniel reached for her, concern written on his bruised face.

"Will you still be my handler?"

He shook his head. "No—"

"I understand." Katie's heart took a gravity plummet into her shoes and her gaze followed. So, she'd be passed along to a stranger. Daniel had made his choice. He had every right to; he shouldn't have to give up his career. She strained to put on a brave expression.

"Chief Bridges will assign you a new handler to avoid a conflict of interest."

Katie jerked to look at Daniel. "A conflict of interest?" she squeaked.

He nodded. "I'll stay on as a marshal until the Marinos' case is closed. For now, he's promised to keep us in the same town while I'm courting you. If you're willing to have me."

She rubbed her arms again, maintaining her distance. His admission, though admirable, would cost him too much. "Daniel, I would never take your ambitions away."

Daniel pushed up from the chair with a groan.

Katie immediately rushed to his side, helping him to stand.

He slid his hands around her waist, pulling her closer, drinking her in with his dark eyes. "Katie, when I thought I'd lost you, I realized that nothing else mattered to me."

"But what about your dreams of making chief..."

"If the only point of my career up to this point was to find you, I'll retire today a happy man. I can always find another job, but I'll never find another Katherine Tribani Isabella Marino. I love you."

Katie's heart danced in her chest. "I love you too."

"I'm so glad we got that settled." Daniel lowered his head, his lips a breath away from hers. "Remember, I can't leave anything unfinished, so you're still stuck with me. If you'll have me."

She grinned. "Promise?"

"I promise." Daniel's hand rested on the back of her head, drawing her to him.

Katie lifted her face, giving him the access he searched for. The kiss was a gentle, sweet caress.

He winced and pulled back. "Sorry, didn't realize that would hurt so much." Daniel put a finger against his swollen, split lip.

Katie laughed. "I'll take a rain check until you're healed."

"Count on it." He grinned and winked, revealing the dimple she'd come to love.

"Does it get better than this?" Katie stayed wrapped in Daniel's embrace, careful not to squeeze too tightly.

"Are you kidding? It only gets better from here."

EPILOGUE

Six months later...

Daniel parked next to the black SUV at the base of the Manitou Incline. His backup had arrived as scheduled and would keep a watchful eye on him and Katie. No worries about an ambush today.

Lush evergreens, bushes and slim trees bordered the path, embracing them with the colors of spring. Couldn't ask for a more beautiful setting. *Wish you were here, Garrett, but I hope I have your blessing.*

"I can't believe it's finally over. No more witness protection. Thanks for the mini-escape before I move to North Carolina." Katie pulled on her backpack. "Though I'd hoped for a nice dinner and a movie. Something a little more romantic."

"What's more romantic than physical exertion? Besides, I need to know you can make the climb again."

"I've already proven I can do it."

"Yeah, but we had killers chasing us."

"Whatever." She gave him a playful poke.

"Ready?"

"Race you."

"Arrogance is a terrible trait."

"Come on, flatlander." Katie glanced over her

shoulder and her grin sent a shiver of delight through Daniel.

They advanced at a steady pace. The jovial bantering slowed as they neared the center of the Incline.

Daniel paused, dropping to rest on a step. "Need. Water."

Katie slid beside him and passed a bottle.

He took a drink and handed it back to her. "You're not even panting."

"A benefit of being younger. I didn't want to point out that elderly man's moving faster than you." Katie gestured toward the gray-haired hiker. "I think he started after us."

Daniel growled, hugging her.

"Careful. This place is full of potential impaling hazards." She giggled.

He pecked her cheek and took the last swig of water. "All right, let's finish this."

"For the record, I'm not the one who needed a break."

He shot her a feigned look of irritation.

They hiked on; words between them became fewer as the climb grew harder.

"We could cut the hike shorter—we're almost to the false summit," Daniel offered.

"Are you kidding? Toughen up, Knight."

He'd created a monster.

Several feet higher, Katie's lighthearted taunting stopped. "Why. Is. It. So. Hard. To. Breathe."

"Because you're still a flatlander."

She pinned him with an emerald glare but didn't stop moving.

When at last they reached the top, they shuffled to the center, reclining under the shade of a sparsely leafed tree.

Nervousness plagued Daniel. *Help me to do this, Lord.*

Katie inhaled. "Mountain air's the best."

"Not many mountains in North Carolina." He wiped his sweaty palms on his pants.

"That's okay. I don't care where we go, as long as you're near. Although I'm not going to lie—I'd love to live here."

"I agree. But with the transfer to the North Carolina office, I'll be able to stay near you and not have to travel as often."

"That's the best part. I still can't believe Priscilla testified and Giovanni confessed to everything."

"He couldn't wait to brag on his nefarious brilliance. He's got no hope of ever getting out of prison."

"I still wish I'd gone to Anthony's funeral."

Daniel pushed down frustration over the topic they'd discussed a hundred different ways. "You couldn't if you wanted to."

"I know..." She stood, looking out over the ridge.

His beautiful day was going south quickly.

Daniel removed the ring box from his backpack, revealing the one-carat round diamond solitaire. With a fortifying breath, he touched her lightly on the shoulder.

Katie turned, her eyes widened and her mouth formed a perfect O as he dropped to one knee in front of her.

Daniel's pulse was so loud in his ears he couldn't hear himself speak. "Katie, since the day you came into my life, I've never been bored or happier. I want a lifetime with you. Will you be my wife?"

Katie nodded with a shimmer of what he hoped were happy tears. "Yes!"

He stood, slipped the ring on her finger and she lunged into his waiting arms. Daniel leaned back, gazing into her eyes. "Promise?"

"I promise."

Daniel lifted his beautiful fiancée's chin, claiming her lips with his. When they finally came up for air, he couldn't resist. He spun Katie in a circle chanting, "We did it. We did it."

* * * * *

Dear Reader,

Thank you so much for sharing Katie and Daniel's story. I often begin writing by asking myself "what if" questions, and *Secret Past* is evidence of that. What if everything I believed was a lie?

Katie's whole world was turned upside down, not just over the loss of her mother, but in discovering her own secret past. She relied on her faith to strengthen her and had to take a leap of faith in trusting Daniel to help her navigate through the lies to find the truth. I love that we have God's voice whispering His truths to us to help us navigate in a world filled with conflicting information. He has promised in Isaiah 30:21, "And thine ears shall hear a word behind thee, saying, This is the way, walk ye in it, when ye turn to the right hand, and when ye turn to the left." I'm so glad God hasn't left us alone to find our way. And one undisputable assurance we have is God's love for each of us.

I enjoy hearing from readers, so please visit me on my website, shareestover.com, or drop me a line at authorshareestover@gmail.com.

Blessings to you,
Sharee